WE CAN'T ALL DIE LIKE BUDDY HOLLY.

JAN SAYER

Jan Sayer has worked with some incredibly exciting people who are far too celebrated to be named in her humble biography. After university, she toured Europe and beyond as a company stage manager and lighting designer.

For ten years, she was a stage manager at Sydney Opera House. She was a producer for the Sydney 2000 Olympic Games and recently an executive assistant at the University of Sydney.

Today she lives on the island of Texel in the Netherlands. She loves cats, sports cars, and the ocean, and she hopes to earn enough to feed her designer clothes habit.

https://jansayer.com

This is a work of fiction. Names, characters, places and incidents are the products of the author's imagination. Any resemblance to actual events, locales or persons, living or dead are entirely incidental.

Copyright © 2022 Jan Sayer

All rights reserved.

No part of this book may be reproduced in any form or by any electronic or mechanical means, including information storage and retrieval systems, without written permission from the author, except for the use of brief quotations in a book review.

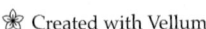

CONTENTS

WEDNESDAY 21 DECEMBER

The body lay perfectly still. The frost had melted and left a slushy pool beneath the corpse. Some small, grey birds flew down and walked around the outstretched hands, regarding them with apprehension. They took a few steps, first in one direction, then in another. They were unsure but not repelled. Death was as irrelevant to them as the breeze that ruffled their feathers. They did not know it, so had no fear of it. Soon they flew away with a faint rustle of wings and the silence returned. The steady drip of the melting ice filled the small garden where the plants, so lovingly tended in warmer days, lay deep in the rich smelling soil. The grass, ragged with brown patches, showed through the wet slush.

The body lay face down in the fishpond with arms fully stretched, as if making a last appeal to an uncaring enemy. The clothes were untouched, simple trousers and knitted sweater that were chosen for comfort and warmth, as were the fur-trimmed slippers on her feet. The day was coming, and the cold air had a faint, hazy quality, almost a beauty.

The garden was separated from its neighbours by a wall of recycled red bricks reclaimed from who knows where. Built long ago, the moss and weeds had begun to dig into small cracks in the mortar. History would undermine this wall just as surely as it would sink or destroy all man-made things. The corpse would in a much shorter time, if not discovered, decay and rot to a yellowing pile of bones. A small ray of sunlight glanced across the watery surface of the lawn. The day was coming, and this quiet killing ground would soon lose its air of mystery and become a squalid scene of horror.

There were sounds now, faint and distant, in the road beyond. Vehicles were coughing their way along the wet streets, crawling reluctantly to the main arteries of the town. The damp air was filling with the poisonous fumes of a world we regard as advanced. So, advanced that humanity is slowly choking itself to extinction and we do nothing. The person on the wet ground no longer cared. What were a few noxious fumes to them now? They were beyond hurt or discomfort. Their troubles were over and wherever their spirit went was anyone's guess. Perhaps it floated high above the polluted land, looking back with disbelief and indifference.

There was a loud, insistent ring. A telephone inside the house rang and then stopped as the answering machine chanted the message. Please leave your name and number and so on. No message. Then it was quiet again and all around, the noises became more varied and intense.

Along the wall, the neighbourhood cat began his daily territorial circuit with a delicate balancing act. Then he stopped and seated himself neatly to groom his fur while he observed the corpse below. As he pushed his whiskers into his sleek cheeks, his eyes never left the ground. He sniffed the wind, looking for clues to the nature of the intruder into his territory. It was too soon for the stench of dead flesh to rise above the cold morning air. He would perhaps note his find and return later before others claimed it. For now, he regarded the body with the detached air of a preoccupied cat.

Soon the thin winter sun was filling the garden. The cat continued to groom himself undisturbed. At the sound of a key in a distant lock, his ears twitched, and his fur rose with apprehension. His body was still like a ghost cat as he waited for sounds of approach. There was a grating sound of a car door closing in the street, and with a twitch of his paws, the cat disappeared silently into the next garden.

Small towns have the same feeling of cold, damp decay, like neglected allotments full of cabbages. Hope left long ago, with the young, the ambitious and the foolhardy. Those in power have, like vampires, drained all the energy into their hearts. Left behind are failure and despair and a faint smell of Brussel sprouts. Communities have died, and people now stay shut in their overpriced houses, afraid of anyone who is a different colour, religion or race. A few things still unite people; banal television programs full of dancing politicians, cooking competitions and talent shows, the results so clearly rigged for profit.

2016 had been a particularly bad year so far. In the America, a madman was in control of the nuclear arsenal. The failure of the left to destroy the evils of social class had simmered and turned to a toxic brew that passed down the food chain. If you are different, you are feared, and no one wants to walk in anyone else's shoes. Children are afraid and are asking questions their parents cannot answer without shame. Young adults are asking, 'why have you let us down' and those who still care are now too depressed to care anymore. The whole country was on a slow slide to the bottom.

Rocky and the Rainbows were also on a long downward slide. Things had not been happening for years, gig-wise. Or money-wise. The excesses of the rock and roll lifestyle got Rocky early on. He was a blonde Californian that they recruited by advertising in NME for a lead singer. With all his Jim Morrison gorgeousness, it did not matter how well he could sing. When he entered a room, all the air was sucked out. He should have tattooed 'Doomed' on his forehead. Once he was gone, the other band members just carried on without him. They were now well over fifty and wore their shirts loose over their increasing waistlines.

Mak was the official bandleader. He was the one with the charm and charisma and the ability to string together more than one sentence while he was still sober. The drummer, Mick, was going deaf, and the bass guitarist, Will, never spoke on stage. It was part of his mystic, he said. Actually, it was his dentures. Occasionally, Peter, the other guitarist, joined them when his wife, Marilyn, allowed him out. If she didn't like him doing a gig, she would turn up with the three kids, and the noise much drowned out the decaying JBL's cranked up to full volume

Once the promoters caught sight of the children smearing ice cream on the already sticky furniture, the set abruptly ended before the band could drink the sixteen beers stipulated by their rider. Now they played the local pub on Saturday nights and the occasional wedding. The Rainbows had hit bedrock.

Mak did not talk much about his financial problems. What could be gleaned from the occasional hint that he dropped was that he had mortgages, a big overdraft, and eight stacked credit cards. He had planned on a hit record that had not happened and lived the rock star life way before he had the financial clout to back it up. Somehow, the gigs got smaller and smaller and now Saturday night at the Leopard was the best there was. He did, however, have a second string to his bow. He was a DJ. Being a DJ became a big thing somewhere in the nineties. Vinyl was dug out of the back of the garage and guys in baseball caps scratched the grooves against the needle of a vintage turntable. This proved to be a lucrative bandwagon to hop on and Mak quickly got the moves and the patter down pat. But somehow, he did not fit the demographic, and so he cornered the market in old school rock and roll.

The boom started in the noughties, and Mak found his

niche. Care homes, third weddings, divorce parties and even funerals. The baby boomers were not going out with 'Ave Maria' and the 'Unchained Melody'. Oh no! They were going out to 'Whole Lotta Love' and Pink Floyd songs. Mak fitted perfectly. He had the lingo; he still had his hair and some cool glasses. On Saturdays, he wriggled into his tightest jeans and relived his past.

His girlfriend, Pattie, was not pleased that day. Her pout could hardly fail to throw a dark pall of gloom over the proceedings. Twice a week she sat in the club and watched Mak do his stuff for the blue-rinses and saggy-waisted. He had not quite lived up to his early promises to her. She had been beautiful then. She was still beautiful in an older sort of way. Still trim, with neatly touched roots to her tousled bed hair. She never married Mak. He was always married to someone else and trying to work it out. Somehow, she never quite left him, even when he turned up drunk on her doorstep, clutching a pawn ticket for his guitar and leather pants. Things were in decline, and she hardly had the energy to stop it.

'So you gonna play this set before they riot?'

She stared at the lethargic crowd intent on their beers and burgers. The communal hall, heated by some ancient, brown painted radiators and the fumes from the kitchen, was a missile target for the local yobs, and the dirty windows were nailed up some years ago as a security measure. The crowd was drowsy from a lack of air and a calorie and fat-sodden meal.

Once the dancing began, the door would be propped open to let in the icy December cold. The hallway was lined with dead-dog or fake-fur trimmed parkas. Fashion was not their priority; fitting into cheap clothes, while consuming chips for every meal, was.

'This lot will be finished eating soon and might want to struggle around the dance floor while they still can. Let's get it over with, shall we?'

She could see that Mak was thinking himself into his rock star persona. His eyes were narrowing, and the second whisky was beginning to work.

'Sure baby doll,' he said.

He did not mean that. Pattie sighed. A rock star would have called her 'baby doll', so he did. Just loud enough for most of the room to hear. Then he hitched his belt higher and headed for the tiny box that doubled as the DJ's stage, now vacated by the bingo caller, and after a gentle tap of the microphone launched into his first track. The dusty turntables remained for effect, and behind them was his laptop that contained all the music. Mak moved with the times and anyway, he never could get the hang of scratching.

The soulful sound of Adele singing 'Set Fire to the Rain' got the audience's attention as they settled their weight down for more beers.

Welcome to Wednesdays with Mak and welcome to everyone out there on Long Time Radio available twenty-four seven on long-timeradio.com. It's quite funny actually, I posted a little link last night on my Facebook page that I was gonna do alphabet rock, cos we all need to learn the alphabet; me probably more than anyone else. I arrive here today, and Pattie has made an alphabet poster of my name that you can see behind me. And she's managed to spell it right. So, a warm, warm welcome to my wonderful Pattie, who is so superb at alphabets. I do know for a fact that she has alphabet spaghetti and alphabet cereal as well. You can get alphabet corn flakes now. She actually thought the cornflakes were a new type of jigsaw puzzle, but when she opened it up, it was all letters.

Pattie flashed a cheery smile from the bar, and Mak responded with a wave. Why the audience believed this shit, she had no idea. She had an idea that it had a lot to do with Mak's charm. He was tall and quite attractive, not a hunk by any stretch of the imagination. He just had a way of making you believe he was a sincere all-round good bloke, instead of a smooth-tongued con-artist who was good at the bullshit. You would trust him to look after your grannie.

Welcome. Obviously, it's all open to requests as per usual, but what I've tried to do is to go through the alphabet; A through to Z obviously beginning with A, even I knew that much, and that was Adele beginning with A. The alphabet. I have to admit that finding all the tunes to run in order and to stay within my two-hour set proved harder than I thought. I did struggle with Q, and I really struggled a lot with X, but I did manage to find them, so I do have the complete alphabet, and according to me, we can do it all within the two hours providing I don't actually say anything. So, let's move straight on to B, and this is Bryan Adams with the 'Summer of Sixty-Nine'.

Mak's voice rose in a flourish as the more active members of the audience waddled onto the dance floor. Pattie took a drink. There were twenty-five songs to go, not counting requests. The more adventurous of the men would be asking her for a dance soon and the thought of their sweaty hands brushing her bum made her feel nauseous. Mak played the tunes, and she supplied the visual delights while she still could. Her master's degree faded like an old bruise. She was only required to be bright and pleasing, like a vase of flowers or a nice table lamp. Even Mak's charms were beginning to make life less than tolerable and watching him juggle the demands of his ex-wife, and her family was wearing her down. Early on, divorce was 'out of the question' because of the children. Ten years later, the needs of the children hardly merited consideration in Pattie's mind, but somehow a divorce never happened. She had a bad feeling that her life was one big con.

7

'Wanna dance, darlin',' said a pimply young man, who leered down the front of her blouse.

Pattie smiled falsely and was led onto the dance floor, and practically groped by her partner. The more she trod on his trainers, the more he grinned. Her torture with several evil smelling men lasted for an hour.

Then she flounced up to the stage and planted a dry kiss on Mak's cheek.

'I will fuckin' kill one of these bastards one of these days,' she hissed into his ear.

Their bodies sagged slightly as both smiled towards the audience. They both cared for each other, but it was fast becoming too much effort to show it. The track ended, and Mak shrugged Patty away with a superficial smile.

So the letter R is represented by a fantastic band that you all know and love. This is Rocky and the Rainbows playing their song of 'Whisky and Wine'.

The audience has heard this track or one like it each week for the last two years. Rocky and Rainbows played well; it is just a bit uninspired, like an undressed salad. As the brief track ended with a Led Zeppelin-inspired twangly bit of guitar that it had taken Mak hours to master, he beamed at his own skill, then switched on the microphone.

A bit of your favourite band there, Rocky and the Rainbows with their hit record, 'Whisky and Wine'. I know I shall see you all on Saturday at the Leopard when I will be donning my rock and roll T-shirt and playing the night away for your delight.

There was a murmur, but it could not be mistaken for delight.

• • •

And now… and now, I can start looking forward to a dance with my lovely lady Pattie as we are on the homeward stretch of the set. Coming up next is S, and that is Stealers Wheel playing your all-time favourite, 'Stuck in the Middle with you'.

Mak's phone rang inside of Pattie's bag. He liked to think of her as his personal assistant.

'Mak's phone. This is Pattie. I can take a message.'

The high-pitched whine of Mak's ex-wife assaulted her ears.

'Tell him that his Aunt Maud ain't answering. I am doing her hair on Friday but she ain't picking up, stupid old bag. He'll have to go round.'

She rang off.

'Goodbye Delia. Have a lovely day.'

Pattie wandered over to the stage and, pretending to give Mak another loving kiss, she said,

'That was your wife. She says you are to go round to your Aunt Maud's. She's not answering her phone, and it's her hair day on Friday.'

'Fuck,' said Mak and quickly reordered his mouth to make it look like he said 'Fine'.

'Thank you, Darlin'', he added for effect.

Back on the dance floor, a group of women was doing what looked like line-dancing in their floppy, fake Ugg boots. A couple of red-faced men were trying to keep up, their fluorescent trainers looking like big white life-boats attached to spindly legs and wobbly bellies. Pattie imagined sleeping next to one of them and quickly closed her eyes to blot out the image. What happens to people, she wondered? A slow descent into lethargy and banality. What happens to hopes and dreams?

• • •

So we've almost come to the end of our little jaunt along the alphabet of life. It kind of made it easy for me. I do hope my choice of tunes was your choice and let's do it all again on Friday with a different alphabet.

Thank you so much to Pattie, and to you all for being here. Now time for me to play you out. So now, we have come to Z. This one wasn't hard, even for me. It's ZZ Top with 'Sharp Dressed Man'.

Then it was time to dance with Pattie. Mak left the stage and took her in his arms so they could jiggle along together. He moved well for a big man and years of dancing together moulded their shapes into one, even if the passion had drained away.

'I have to go to Maud's. Will you come with me?'

'Like hell I will. Miserable old cow and the house stinks. She is your Aunt. Sort it yourself. I got stuff to do.'

'I'll take your car then?'

'You will not. I'll drive you back, and then you go in your own car.'

The club voyeurs watched the couple dance comfortably in each other's arms and most reflected that Pattie and Mak had done well for themselves. Good-looking couple. Most were not that lucky.

When the doors were thrown open and the cold air washed in, Mak was assaulted by the wobbly bodies of his female admirers as they pushed themselves against him and pecked him on the cheek. He could feel their chubby fingers wandering into the pockets of his jeans to get a quick feel as they slipped in a five-pound note. His only male fan gave him a manly hug and pushed a £10 note into his back pocket while pushing his fingers towards Mak's arse. Mak wanted to punch him, but he needed the money rather badly. His mortgage payments were overdue this month.

In the heady days of potential stardom, he had bought two houses. Neither was fully paid for. His ex-wife Delia, often known as Dearest, lived in one , and his kids used the other as a squat. He and Pattie lived in a top floor rented flat with no lift. Pattie squeezed his hand when it was time to go. He smiled and was thankful for her warmth as they picked up his gear and walked towards the car.

'Do you know what's up with Aunt Maud?' Pattie asked once they were in the car.

'No idea. Dearest does her hair Friday, and if she is not answering the phone, I should go round and check on the old girl. I really can't be bothered to run round after my relatives.'

'But you will, won't you? If you don't, you wife will shout at you over the phone and then come round and hassle you some more cos you don't do as you are told. You just don't have the knack of standing up for yourself unless you are rat arsed.'

Mak looked sad for a moment and then decided that Pattie looked rather nice today. She was in her fifties, but still had her curves and her pretty mouth. He liked that pretty mouth; it had mysterious skills. He was tired, and a nap before facing Maud's place was on his mind.

Once in the flat, he grabbed Pattie and pushed her against the wall. This was Pattie's cue to be friendly, and she threw off her jacket while fumbling with his zip.

Sometimes, if she caught Mak at the right time, the sex could be quite pleasant if the hydraulics worked. She felt around until her hand found something that felt like a limp sausage. She massaged a bit without much success. Mak was looking hopeful, so they manoeuvred towards the bedroom and struggled out of their clothes.

Once on the bed, they realised that was rather cold and, pulling the duvet over themselves, tried for some heavy petting. This was Mak's best move, and he had practised fingering on hundreds of groupies in his rock and roll days. There was never time to fuck them all, and some of them didn't look too clean. Pattie, on the other hand, was deliciously clean. She smelled and tasted nice.

Pattie was now grappling with the flaccid sausage. She slid down the bed and regarded Mak's cock with amusement.

'Hello little dick,' she said, chuckling.

It was not large, but it was nice and pink and balanced neatly on a bed of sliver pubic hair. As it lay limply in her hand, she wondered how long it was going to take to get it into a condition to penetrate her. She took it into her mouth and began to roll her tongue around the tip. Mak groaned appreciatively and ruffled her hair. After ten minutes, Pattie was sure this was not to be the satisfying fuck she was hoping for, so she clamped her teeth around his cock and bit him. Not hard, but just hard enough to let him know she was over it. Mak yelped, and Pattie wriggled up to face him.

'You are gonna have to get that fixed, Mak.'

'Sorry,' said Mak and rolled over.

They lay there for a while, not speaking until Mak fell asleep. Pattie slid out of bed, put on her warmest dressing gown, and went to see why the flat was cold. She had paid the bill. Mak could not be trusted with that. She switched the heating up a notch, but the flat was still artic, and there was not going to be much in the way of sex to warm her up. She made some tea and sat in front of the gas fire, trying not to weep for her lost life.

It was nine o'clock when Mak woke up. Pattie had made dinner, and the two ate in silence while the TV droned on in the background. They had already said everything they needed to say to each other, and the conversation revolved around the day-to-day problems, like when Mak lost something and he had to explain to Pattie. Pattie controlled the finances for the flat, so the rent was paid, and the electricity and gas stayed connected.

There was no room for extras. Pattie worked at home doing the books for a couple of local firms, including Delia's hairdressing business. Badly named as Dearests Dos, the painted sign was apostrophe-free, as it was not the tradition in that area to place too much store on punctuation. Nor reading or writing, for that matter. Literacy did not feature on most people's wish list, whereas a large screen TV certainly did. It was a hand to mouth economy, and the stuff that went in the mouth soon showed on the hips.

'Damn,' said Mak as he settled down to watch the football. 'I forgot Maud.'

He did not seem overly concerned. His Aunt Maud was a robust woman in her late seventies. Not likely to fall down dead any time soon. Pattie curled up on the sofa for a few minutes and snuggled up to Mak.

'Do it tomorrow, luv. I'll ignore the phone. Delia won't come round in this weather. She might get her new suede boots messy. Then where would we be?'

Mak smiled and turned back to his sport. Pattie thought he looked very tired and pale. It was not the moment to have a serious talk about selling the houses and shedding the enormous burden of his ex-wife and ungrateful kids.

Delia would get half, or more if she could bully Mak into giving it to her. She certainly would try. Pattie had never met anyone quite so entitled as Delia. She could not understand why Mak put up with it. He was unfaithful to Delia all through their stormy marriage, so she supposed it was guilt. By now, he should have paid for his sins twice over. She pecked him on the cheek and went to bed, knowing that he would fall asleep in front of the TV.

———

FRIDAY 23 DECEMBER

Friday morning, it was freezing hard. Sunday was Christmas Day, and Mak had to prepare his sets for the bingo for the next week. Same old stuff as last year would probably work. Pattie thought if she heard Slade's 'Merry Xmas Everybody', again, she might cut her throat. He always finished with The Pogues song, 'Fairytale of New York'. It summed up their life perfectly, just one big shouting match and lots of failed make-up sex.

She took Mak his coffee and settled down at her computer to do the accounts. The work was easy, and she made enough money to pay the bills and to squirrel a bit away for herself. Money was best kept a long way away from Mak, who lived from one nasty call from his creditors to the next. He liked Pattie to answer the phone and take messages, so he didn't have to deal with the frustrated callers.

Somehow, each month, he managed to pay his considerable mortgage payments. He had suggested that Delia might take over the payments for her house and he would sign it over to her, but as Delia managed to keep her hairdressing business operating by just covering the business costs and not showing a profit; she didn't want a mortgage. The profit went firmly into Delia's back pocket in cash. Any suggestion of a sale was met with a campaign of hysterical crying, and a return of a mysterious illness that the doctors could not quite put their fingers on.

The second house was a complete mess. If Mak mentioned that he wanted to sell Delia accused him of child cruelty. Mak saw little of his son and daughter, and he preferred it that way. He failed them, and he knew it. So Delia continued to have the upper hand, and Mak was simply not strong enough to oppose her. Pattie was only the 'girlfriend' as far as Delia was concerned. She was his wife.

Mak looked very pale when he wandered into the room with his empty cup.

'You all right Mak?'

'I feel a bit sick. That late-night band practice is catching up on me'.

The Rainbows tried to rehearse once a week, but usually, it was just a prolonged drinking session in the drummer's garage. Tuesday night they had all passed out on the old sofas in front of the electric fire, and Mak had not returned home until he was sober enough to drive the next morning.

'You want anything to eat?'

Mak shook his head.

'If I don't eat it, I don't throw it up, do I? I will make another coffee and go back to bed until it's time.'

'What about Maud?'

'Screw Maud.'

Delia tried several times the previous day to call Aunt Maud without success. She was 'put out', as she called it. She had a business to run. She did not have time to check on his Aunt Maud. She dressed with her usual care and still managed to look like a prime suspect for the fashion police.

At 10am, she arrived at her shop and opened up. The junior, Paulina, was standing on the doorstep shivering and holding a carton of milk.

She had been the junior for two years, and that did not seem likely to change. She was poorly trained, so it was not likely she would find another job.

Dearests Dos was cheap, and people got what they paid for, which was a few streaks, and wash and blow dry. Or a blow job as Delia liked to call it. The customers had stopped giggling at that one some years ago. Delia unlocked, and Paulina went to put the kettle on. Delia teased her hair and touched up her lipstick. Then she tried one more time to call Aunt Maud. As there was no answer, she called Mak's mobile, intending to shout at whoever answered. Pattie did not intend to answer any calls, and her own mobile number was a closely guarded secret.

Delia swore and went to check the day's appointments. There were four that morning, the usual fortnightly pensioner wash and sets and a child's cut. The only appointment that afternoon was at 3pm. That was a teenage girl who would be quite happy to have her hair done by Paulina. They could gossip about the difference between blue and green streaks.

'No appointments for me after lunch today, Paulina,' she shouted to the kitchen. 'I have to go see his Aunt Maud.'

'Righty oh,' Paulina shouted back as she back-combed her hair in the big mirrors.

Mak finally got up about one o'clock and Pattie made him a sandwich and cup of tea while he showered and dressed. He still looked ill, and Pattie was concerned but said no more about it. He was still a looker. His hair was a lovely mishmash of silver and black. It curled around his ears. Pattie thought it was great to see a man of his age with lots of hair. Good genes, she guessed. His eyes were wide and grey, and he wore fashionable glasses with red sidepieces and little logos. There was a slight tint to the lenses. Mak, mindful of his rock and roll image, would have preferred to wear dark glasses, but in England, he found he was groping around in the dark so gave up trying.

He was taller than Pattie, taller than most men, which she liked about him. His waistline was starting to spread, but as it was fashionable to wear loose t-shirts, he could still hide the bulges for now at least.

But it was Mak's voice that made women love him. If it was a colour, then it was rich brown, soft and friendly. You could hear the smile in it. Sometimes you could hear the pain, too. He chuckled a lot, which made you want to hug him.

He was articulate, funny and self-deprecating. He warmed hearts and tugged at heartstrings. Sometimes, Pattie closed her eyes and felt as if she was listening to the man she first fell in love with. He was still there in that voice, even if the man had become defeated and sour. If the devil spoke, he would sound like Mak. They arrived at the bingo club half way through the games and settled down at the bar to wait until the break.

'Hungry Mak?' asked the barmaid, showing him what was on offer.

Mak tried not to stare too hard as two enormous breasts were pointed in his direction.

'Regrettably, I am not hungry,' Mak replied diplomatically.

'Can I get some wedges please?' Pattie asked.

The barmaid looked Mak over and then slowly turned to Pattie.

'Make you fat, darlin', she said hopefully.

'I'm sure I can cope,' Pattie replied, as she claimed Mak's attention from his admirer.

'What do I say to Delia if she phones while you are doing the set?'

'Tell her I'm dead or better still, tell her I have lost my memory and can only speak Portuguese. Perhaps she will fuck off then.'

'She will only fuck off, as you put it, when you find the balls to tell her. Until then, the mother of your children will hang like a dead weight around both our necks until we die. Or alternatively, she does, whichever comes first.

'Quit bitching,' Mak snapped sourly.

'Not bitching, Mak. Telling you like it is. The day will come very soon when either she is out of your life, or I am. Understand?'

Mak pretended to be occupied looking around the room. Selective deafness was his favourite defence these days. One day, thought Pattie, I shall write it on the bathroom mirror in huge lipstick letters so you can't avoid it. As for leaving Mak, she had tried but failed. Love sometimes makes you stick like glue to the wrong person.

She just hoped that the kids moved on soon and at least one of the houses could be sold to relieve the pressure. Janis, who was the eldest, lived in the terrace house with her occasional boyfriends, names unknown as they changed frequently. Surely, she would want to move away soon. Go backpacking or whatever they did these days.

Joe was just twenty and would be less easy to shift. He was unemployed and, Pattie thought, dealing in the odd bit of blow to pay for his toys. Going home to his mother would not be something he would relish. Pattie secretly hoped he would get busted and spend enough time with Her Majesty so Mak could sell the house. The kids had been brought up by Delia and thought the world owed them a living, and free holidays. Mak just felt guilty that he had not been around.

By the time, Mak was ready to start his set, he had already downed two neat whiskies; large ones as the barmaid pushed the optics more than once when she served him. He plugged in his laptop and checked his microphone. Once everyone settled down, he began.

. . .

Hey, good afternoon everybody, and Happy Friday, of course, to everyone out there tuned into Long Time Radio for the next two hours at least, I hope. Special welcomes, of course, to all of you. Lots of people here today. This is most delightful and exciting. Some of you I know and some of you I don't.

Now, as I do every time, I got a few tunes that I'm gonna play, but if there is anything that you'd like to listen to, then give me a shout, and I'll do whatever I can. I can play something that you might want to dedicate to somebody you love or at least feel very strongly about. Or perhaps you desperately want to hear something that you haven't heard for a long time. Or maybe you just want to poke fun at someone by playing them a special tune. I can do it all.

All you have to do is tell my lovely Pattie at the bar. Easy peasy. In the meantime, here's a bit of Teresa James. This is 'The Wind Cries the Blues'.

His voice was so alive, so full of fun, but his face was drawn, and his smile switched off as soon as he closed the mic. Mak was not well or maybe very worried.

Delia, meanwhile, was on her way to Aunt Maud's. The morning had been busy, and Paulina would deal with the one afternoon client and had strict instructions to lock up and deliver the keys to Delia's house on her way home. She trusted Paulina with scissors, but not the keys to the shop. She drove to Aunt Maud's house, which was a rather nice semi on a new housing estate. Delia wondered where the money had come from for that house. Maud did not work, so the house must be paid off. She had an idea that Maud's husband had done something for the council. Hand in the till, she expected. The street was empty as most people were not yet home from work and she reversed easily into a free space.

After a few minutes of ringing the bell, Delia wondered if Maud had gone out. She peered through the front window. It was impossible to see inside because of the thick, unattractive net curtains. The neighbour opposite crossed the road to see what she was doing and, recognising Delia, asked if anything was wrong.

'Have you seen Maud today?'

'No, ducks. Not seen her this week. Oh, wait, I did see her on Tuesday, I think, fetching her fags. Could have been Monday. Why summant wrong?'

'She's not answering her phone,' said Delia.

'We better go round the back then,' said the man. 'Maybe she had a fall and can't get up.'

Delia thought there was little chance of Mak's Aunt Maud falling over unless soundly drunk.

The two went along the side passage, and the man reached over and took the bolt off the gate. It was very cold, and Delia had left her fleecy hoodie in her car. There was an extension at the back of the house, with glass doors opening onto the scrubby lawn.

Delia walked around the corner of the glass box while the neighbour hung about in the gateway. He was having second thoughts about getting involved and, like most men, hung back, non-committal. What Delia saw first were two arms stretched out beyond the open glass doors. Aunt Maud was lying face down on the paving at the end of the lawn. Around her head was a flock of crows.

Delia stood for a minute, taking in the scene. The first thing that crossed her mind before the shock sank in was that this was a very nice house and must be worth a few bob. Then she moved closer and could see exactly what the birds were feasting on. She had seen a lot of murder mysteries; she knew what to do next. Taking a deep breath, she opened her painted mouth and screamed as dramatically as she could. The neighbour came running. He grabbed Delia by the arm and pulled her back to the gateway. She looked pale.

'Got your phone, ducks?'

Delia gulped down the nausea and hunted in her bag. She

stood looking at it for a moment and then dialled Mak's number.

'Call the police, ducks - call 999,' the neighbour said helpfully.

At the other end, Pattie fished Mak's phone out of her bag. She listened to the gibberish on the other end, and seeing by the display, which showed a picture of a dragon, that it was Delia calling, she waited until the shrieking stopped.

'Calm down, Delia, and tell me in plain English, if that is possible, what exactly the problem is.'

Delia started up again, and Pattie heard the phone move wildly around as she pointed towards the body and then tried again to speak.

'Delia! Breathe!'

Pattie waited.

'Now tell me clearly what is wrong.'

By now, most of the club were aware that something dramatic was happening and settled down to listen to the one side of the conversation. Mak, returning from the gents, and hitching up his jeans, sensed all was not right and stopped just far enough away so Pattie could not hand the phone to him. Pattie listened carefully as Delia finally blurted out that Maud was dead, and birds were pecking at her face and that she felt faint and was about to be sick.

'Delia, why are you calling us, you stupid woman? Call the police. Now!'

Mak was just staring at her as Pattie ended the call. Those in earshot were waiting for more information, but they were out of luck. Pattie put her arms around Mak's neck and said firmly in his ear.

'Get your gear. We are leaving now. Don't say anything, you hear? I'll tell you in the car.'

She crossed the bar to the bingo caller, who was also the promoter.

'Mak's had a death in the family. He has to leave now.'

'Is he expecting to get paid?'

'He fucking is, you heartless moron.'

Once in the car, Pattie explained quietly that Delia had found his Aunt Maud dead.

'I told her to call the police. We better go and see what has happened. I'm so sorry, love.'

'Why?' Mak looked puzzled. 'You didn't kill her, and I can't say she was my favourite Aunt.'

He reached for a flask in the glove compartment and took a gulp.

'She was your only Aunt.'

'Yea well. She didn't make a huge impression on the affection scale, so to speak. Just a relative and I got too many of those, haven't I?'

Pattie looked at her lover for a moment. Shock talking. He is still processing the information. She drove slowly to a café a few streets away and hauled Mak out of the car and made him drink a strong black coffee with lots of sugar. They sat for about ten minutes in silence.

'Tell me why we are sitting here?' Mak asked.

'Because we are waiting for the police to arrive and get everything under control before we appear on the scene. I hope that they will sedate Delia and we can deal with this calmly. Anyway, she is your Aunt so let's hope Delia can be removed so things can be done without the drama and hysteria.'

'What did she say happened? Heart attack?'

'She didn't say, really. Just kept going on about birds eating her face and shrieking. Sounded like she died in the garden. It was a performance worthy of Midsomer Murders. Let's hope they keep her away from the newspapers. She is your Aunt, so Delia can just back off.'

'Will I have to bury her and things?'

'Not personally, love, but I expect you will have to sort out the funeral. There's no one else, is there?'

'Will I have to identify her?' Mak looked rather green.

'I doubt it. Delia seems to have done that already.'

Mak sat staring at the empty cup. He looked so vulnerable; Pattie could have hugged him. Surely he could cope with this, not leave everything to her for once.

They drove to the house, and there was already a police constable stationed outside the front gate. On the other side of the road, an ambulance had parked with back doors open. The constable stopped Pattie and Mak at the gate.

'This is Mrs Bett's nephew,' Pattie explained. 'We were called.'

The constable opened the gate and let them in.

'Wait here please.'

He turned and walked around the side of the house towards the back gate.

'KC, next of kin is here,' he called out.

He returned to them and asked their names and assuming Pattie was Mak's wife, wrote Mrs in his book, which Pattie corrected.

'It's Ms, and I am Mak's partner. Mrs Mason is his ex-wife. She found the body, I believe.'

The constable looked puzzled.

'She called us first. I told her to call you, which obviously, she did.'

The constable smiled at Pattie. She seemed quite in control. He liked women who did not make a fuss.

'Ok, if you folks would wait here, the Inspector will talk to you soon.'

He disappeared with their details, leaving them freezing in the front garden. They moved to the porch and sheltered out of the cold. Finally, a man in a long overcoat came around the side of the house and looked for them. Finding them huddled in the porch, he opened the door and led them into the front room. In the rooms beyond, they could hear voices and movement.

'Sit down,' he said, looking around. 'Too many glass animals for my taste,' he added, smiling at them.

He was used to dealing with these situations, but this was the next of kin, and certain niceties had to be observed. Mak and Pattie sat on the slimy leather-look sofa. He looked at his notepad and then established who they were before he got down to formally breaking the sad news, which they knew anyway.

'I am Detective Inspector Colley, Kit Colley, also known as KC and young for my rank before you comment. I will be heading up this investigation. I'm what they call a high flying, fast track officer. Just so you know,' he added, smiling.

'You are Makenzie Mason, the nephew of Mrs Maud Betts, and this is Ms Pattie Harding, your partner. Mrs Delia Mason, sometimes known as Dearest, is your ex-wife and she discovered your Aunt's body.'

He waited as if they might disagree. No one did.

'I think I am right that you are Mak Mason, the guitarist?'

Mak nodded.

'I hope I may call you Mak. And you can call me KC. I do things my way and formalities seem to get in my way, you understand. And may I call you Pattie?'

He asked kindly, looking directly into her eyes.

Pattie smiled. He was so gentle. It was as if he was taking her out to dinner. About forty or so, she guessed, but looking a lot younger and very fit. Short cropped hair and unshaven. Dark suit and thin tie under a long black coat. Army and Navy store, she thought. A bit of a Keanu Reeves. Neat, tidy, with stunning blue eyes; one a bit droopy under black lashes, like he'd been punched some time ago. Pattie would have given him a second look in a different situation.

'Now Mak and Pattie, if I understand correctly, you were called by Mrs Mason when she discovered the body and you,

Pattie, told her to call the police. Am I right? You were at the bingo club where you work, and you came here directly after the call.'

'Correct,' said Pattie, not intending to mention the stop for coffee.

'And Mak, the deceased is your father's sister, Mrs Maud Betts. The woman who discovered the body, Mrs Delia Mason, was coming round to do Mrs Bett's hair. Do I have this right?' he asked Mak.

'Yes. She wanted me to check on Maud yesterday, but I ran out of time with working and things. Dearest said Maud was not answering the phone and I should go round and check. She was a strong old lady, so I didn't worry. My ex is a bit of a hysteric as you will have seen.'

Detective Inspector Colley smiled knowingly at Mak. He didn't regard woman as any more hysterical than men, and he had seen a lot of hysterical men in his profession.

'Yes, we saw, Mak. So, you had no reason to be concerned about your Aunt then. Her health was good, etc. When did you last see her then?'

Mak paused and looked at Pattie for help.

'Early this week,' said Pattie. 'You dropped off the toaster we picked up from Argos for her.'

Mak nodded.

'Tuesday or Wednesday, was it?'

'Tuesday,' confirmed Pattie. 'You were going to band practice straight after.'

'Right,' said Mak. 'Tuesday tea time then.'

KC made notes and seemed happy with the information. He did not rush, took his time and got everything just right. He was getting to the difficult bit now.

'Now your Aunt, Mak, died suddenly, sometime early Wednesday morning, we think. We can't tell yet, of course, but that is as close as the pathologist can get right now. The cause of death may be natural. She may have had a stroke or cardiac arrest. We will know later today. Nevertheless, as with any unwitnessed death, we have to check on things. Right now, no reason to be suspicious. The body had been lying uncovered in the garden for more than twenty-four hours. Her face has sustained some damage.'

Mak looked alarmed, and Pattie thought he might be sick.

'No need for you to identify the body, Mak. Your ex-wife has done that already. Try not to think about it. She was already at peace.'

Pattie held Mak's hand tightly for a moment, but her eyes were on KC. He had this way of making you pay attention. Soft, firm voice. He was intelligent, and he knew it, and it showed. He was in complete control.

'Now,' said KC, 'I hope I can leave it to you to inform other family members. I believe you have two grown-up children, Mak. They have taken your ex-wife to the Infirmary for a check-up, but it is just shock. She will recover.'

His voice gently implied that the police were enjoying the quiet now Delia was removed and being sedated.

'So, people, go home and have a hot sweet cup of tea or something stronger. Your Aunt is at peace, and we will take care of things from here. We will see you when the autopsy is complete, and we know the cause of death.'

Pattie stood up and took Mak's arm.

'Thanks, err, KC. You have been very kind. We will go home.'

'Is your band playing on Saturday night, Mak?' asked KC as they approached the door.

'Yes, usually do,' said Mak, looking dazed by the question.

'I might come down and listen. It's been a while since I heard a live band. Play your Aunt a farewell song, eh?'

'He will,' said Pattie, as she led Mak to the car.

It was dark when Pattie and Mak got home. The flat was cold and bleak. Neither of them bothered with Christmas decorations. The rest of the block had gone overboard as usual, and the flashing reindeer on the balcony kept everyone awake. Even the hookers on the second floor had lots of bright red bows and tinsel in their windows. Pattie heated up some Bolognese sauce and boiled some spaghetti. They drank the remains of some red wine and said little. Mak was silent and slumped in front of the TV while Pattie washed up and then had her bath.

Mak called the band to confirm the gig was on for Saturday night. He read off the set list. He had added a bit of tribute to his Aunt Maud.

'Who?' asked Mick, who was the deaf drummer. Mak was never sure if he did not hear, or it was just Mick's little joke.

Will, the bass player, was enthusiastic. He liked Christmas gigs. Mak, on the other hand, hated them. Sentimental shit. Next, he called Peter's landline. He was unsure if Peter's wife intended to let him out.

'Hi Marilyn,' he said brightly, assuming she would answer the phone and not Peter, who was usually at work.

'I expect you heard about my Aunt, luv.'

He was playing the sympathy card first, as Marilyn usually said yes if he approached her right. She said yes that night in Leeds when he propositioned her after the gig.

'Look, Marilyn, we really want Peter to play tomorrow for the Christmas gig, and I really want you to be there, too. I miss seeing your smiling face on band nights.'

He could sense she was listening.

'Look darlin'. How about if I pay for you and the kids to have a meal in the Cubs restaurant while Peter plays? Then the kids can hear their Dad, and you can dress up pretty and have a night out. I will even stand you a taxi home. What do you say?'

Marilyn was thinking about how far she might push this offer.

'Can I bring my Mum too?'

Damn you, thought Mak.

'Sure darlin', love to see her. How is she, good, eh?'

'She is just fine Mak, thanks for asking.'

'Ok Marilyn, I will see you and Mum and the kids about seven. Looking forward to it?'

Marilyn said that would be nice, having secured a night out and a free meal and taxi home.

Then he sent a text to Peter, who was still at work.

M YES 2 GIG SAT

Later, Mak joined Pattie in bed. He rolled her over and ran his hands over her breasts and stomach.

'Not tonight, Mak,' she said wearily.

'Comfort fuck maybe,' Mak said hopefully and pushed his fingers into her dry cunt.

'Get off Mak. I'm tired.'

'Oh go on, Pattie. Make me smile,' he said, pushing harder and trying to kiss her.

Pattie had had enough for one day.

'Get off me, Mak. I'm worn out.'

Mak retreated.

The silence hung over the bed for ten minutes, and Pattie hoped he had fallen asleep.

Then he said, 'You tired of me, Pattie?'

'I am tired of this life, and I am tired of your damned family, Mak. They drain the money out of you and the life out of me. Can we please get Aunt Maud buried and then leave?'

'I suppose I will get the house,' said Mak, sounding hopeful. 'Dearest will want some, of course.'

'Fuck, Dearest,' protested Pattie angrily, turning over to face him. 'Sell the houses and pay off your debts. Then divorce her, and we can leave.'

'And go where?' Mak asked sadly. 'Too late for me to start again. My career is over. I'm too old for this business.'

'Rubbish Mak, you are not too old. You still play good, and you are a good DJ. Let's go to Portugal or somewhere and get you a job on a Brit radio station. Somewhere warm for me, where growing old don't hurt so much.'

'I don't see why you are still here, Pattie,' he said, looking at her. 'You are clever. You could have done so much better; have a nice home, couple of kids, not a broken-down old rocker who cannot get it up. You should have left me years ago.'

'I should have, but I didn't. Go to sleep, Mak. The next few days won't be pretty. I suppose Delia will tell the kids about Maud?'

'Expect so. She'll tell anyone who will listen. Kids won't care. They never visited the old girl. Janis might think she's getting a share. I expect Maud has left it to the cat's home.'

'She didn't like cats, and you are her nearest family, Mak, and you did a lot of things for her. Stands to reason, she has left you her house. Sell it, and things might look a bit brighter for us.'

'Hope so, hun.'

Mak smiled his slow smile, the one she loved best. The smile that kept her with him. It started in the corners of his mouth and spread evenly to the whole of his face. You could hear that smile when he talked. He sighed and rolled over. Pattie had the idea that once he was over the shock, he would not mourn much for his Aunt Maud. Poor old cow.

———

SATURDAY 24 DECEMBER

The next day, an ornate black-edged notice on a piece of A4 paper was stuck to the door of Dearests Dos.

OPENING LATE DUE TO FAMILY BEREAVEMENT

Paulina had shown off her computer skills by making the sign edged with black bows. She had used a template for a party invitation, but the printer only had a black cartridge, so it worked out rather well. She rearranged Delia's appointments. It was Christmas Eve, so the salon would be busy in the afternoon. Delia was certain she would feel 'strong' enough to come in. Her daughter, Janis, who Delia bullied into staying the night in case support was needed, took her a hot cup of tea in bed that morning.

'Yeah right,' said Janis, 'like you ever needed support. And don't forget you are doing my hair for free, too.'

Delia wondered about her children. They seemed cold somehow. She assumed they took after Mak.

'Would you get out all my black dresses, Janis, luv? I shall need them for next week. I wonder if we should take the Christmas decorations down.'

'Gawd,' said Janis, helping herself to a dab of the Chanel

'Mademoiselle' from the dressing table.

Detective Inspector Kit Colley was tying up the loose ends before Christmas. He studied the notes on the Aunt Maud's death, then put in a call to the pathologist.

'Anything for me yet?' He asked hopefully.

The pathologist at the other end reeled off the findings.

'Death was about between midnight on Tuesday and 4am on Wednesday morning. The deceased had drunk more than three standard measures of wine, that disgusting pink fizzy stuff we sell to masses these days. Her last meal was some hours earlier and consisted of fish and chips, onion rings and mushy peas, so a cordon blue diet, I think. Damage to face and eyes due to the hungry crows. The victim drowned.'

He paused for a reaction, and when there was none, he continued.

'People can drown in as little as 30mm of water lying face down. She must have fallen or blacked out and landed face down in the little fishpond. Very little water enters the lungs in the early stages of drowning, then a small amount of water in the trachea causes a muscular spasm, and that seals the airway until unconsciousness occurs. You can't shout or call for help, as you can't get enough air. Then goodnight Auntie Maud.'

'So what was she doing in the garden on a cold night?'

'Calling the cat? That is your job. From this end, it was a straightforward case of a drunken old lady falling over and drowning in the garden pond. Damn things should have a fence round them.'

'So nothing for us, then? She wasn't pushed or held down?'

'No sign of it, so we can release the body once all the tests are concluded. I don't think we will find anything. I'll leave the next of kin to you, and you can have a restful Christmas.'

'Thanks,' said KC.

Not quite what he had expected, but less paperwork to do.

KC was not the stereotype detective; he did not have a drink, gambling, wife, family, girlfriend or a weight problem. He was not disillusioned with the police force. On the other hand, he was not stupid enough to believe he was 'making a difference'. He had jumped at a career that paid his university fees and provided him with a good basic pay. It was interesting and challenging. Once his superiors got used to his relaxed style and his obvious talent, they settled down, got off his back and let him get on with it. His team respected him. He was clear and fair and went the extra mile himself and did not dump the shit jobs on them as so many senior officers did.

KC did not kid himself that his job was for life. He lived simply in a one-bedroom flat. He had a regular stream of girlfriends from outside of the police force and did not mix business with pleasure. His mum had moved to Spain some ten years ago, and his plan was to work until he was ready for a change and then base himself close by and help her run her bar. Being a detective inspector paid well, sounded exciting, had its moments, but it was not for life. Not his life, anyway.

It was Christmas Eve. He stared at the sparsely decorated tree on the other side of the office and sighed. Nothing planned for Christmas, as usual. His current girlfriend was on holiday in the Algarve with her family, so it was tinned Christmas pudding and a bottle of wine in front of his computer. He thought he would spend the evening at The Leopard. This large rambling old pub provided the only live entertainment for miles around. The landlord had opened up the tiny, old-fashioned bars and made a big space with a stage for bands.

A cute restaurant called Cubs divided the families from the drinkers and boosted the turnover. It was 'family friendly', which meant you could dump the kids at a table with a plate of chicken nuggets, so they did not run riot in the main bar and disturb the serious drinkers. The men got pissed, and the wives drove home. It was everything about British society that KC hated, but he did like the music. He would take a look at the Rainbows. They played well once, so he expected they were still worth hearing. Strictly speaking, he should not pass on the news about Aunt Maud, of course. That could wait until it was official. Accidental death, death by misadventure, whatever. He could have a night out and pass on his condolences. That was okay, no harm in that. He expected Pattie would like some company, too.

That afternoon, the salon was busy as usual, with Delia squeezed into a tight black tunic and leggings, graciously accepting the condolences of all her customers. A candle surrounded by some fake flowers from an old window display burnt on a small pedestal table containing a few cards, one from Paulina and one which Delia had bought herself and signed with an illegible signature.

As one of the clients remarked, 'It must have been such a shock, Dearest. It is nice to have some cards even though she wasn't really blood, was she?'

Delia pretended not to hear this. She tried to cultivate the sort of poise that she had seen portrayed in Downton Abbey, which she followed religiously. She cut out pictures of the character's hairstyles and put them up in a tasteful wall display under a sign saying, 'Elegant Hairstyles for Weddings'. So far, no one had requested any of these styles because they were too flat. Delia's customers like their hair to have height, by which they meant back-combed to resemble a bird's nest.

Today, both she and Paulina were very busy with the cuts and styles. Janis was doing the wash and head massage and would be paid considerably more than Paulina for her time. This allowed Delia to attend to the important clients and, as she told them, it was comforting to have her daughter by her side 'at this terrible time'. She was milking Aunt Maud's death for all the sympathy she could get and was hoping some customers might send flowers, which she could take home for Christmas. She did not suppose Mak would be inclined to send any. She was telling everyone what a dreadful shock finding the body had been, when honestly she saw little more than a shape laying on the floor and few birds by the pond. She wondered if she might get compensation for her distress, but was unsure who might provide this.

Mak got up at lunchtime. He had drunk rather a lot of whisky on the previous night, as he feared he might not sleep. He thought he might have nightmares, but was so exhausted, he just slept. Pattie made him a big breakfast, and at about eleven o'clock drove him to the Leopard to unload the gear and then went off to do her shopping. She had seen enough band set-ups to last her a lifetime. She had to sell t-shirts before the set, and that was enough for her.

Mick, the deaf drummer, arrived with his gear and the rest of the band's battered equipment. Will, the bass guitarist, who still nursed a dream that one day they would be big stars, followed him in. The landlord's son, who liked to call himself a sound engineer, wandered in, plugged them into the pub's PA system, and checked the microphones. He dumped the three dusty fold-back monitors at the front of the stage. Once he had secured the microphones into the old stands with gaffer tape, he set up the sound desk and did a sound check.

Then he turned off the PA, so the afternoon drinkers were not disturbed, and the three musicians did a few warm-up tunes and discussed the play list. Peter would arrive in the evening with his family, simply plug into the tuner pedal, check his guitar and then play. He had long since given up his dreams of stardom. On the outside, the equipment looked very shabby. The amplifiers had seen a lot of road miles and careless roadies, but most worked well still.

Mak's amp needed replacing, but that had to wait. He had three guitars left from the days when things looked promising; a standard red Stratocaster, that was expensive even back then, and an old Gibson acoustic with an add-on electric pick up. But his pride and joy was a vintage 1930s National Resonator, with its distinctive metal body. Pattie joked that one day she would put his ashes in it. The guitars were scuffed and faded but were locked in the storeroom between the setup and the gig. Mak was not under the illusion his guitars might be stolen by a devoted fan. More like a drug crazed junkie needing some cash. The insurance had run out a long time ago. When they completed the fiddly task of blu-tacking the spare picks to the microphone stands and the three friends settled down to jam comfortably. They had been through a lot together and had stories to share that they dare not tell the women in their lives.

Mak had no idea how many women there had been. Even when he was married to Delia, there was a different one every week. He was an old-school misogynist. He did not see that it was wrong to fuck as many women as he could and, given his considerable charms, there were many ready to fall for them. He told them lies and dumped them the following week. He did not see it as wrong, just part of the rock and roll lifestyle.

When he left Delia, and moved in with Pattie, it was clear that she would not stand for this and he needed her now to keep his chaotic life under control. At most gigs, some woman would make him an offer, but Pattie was on hand to see that it was refused. He no longer had the energy for sex; even though he kidded himself he was still good at it. It was better to give them a kiss on the cheek and decline the offer rather than rumours of his less than sparkling sexual performance be all around the town the following week.

Pattie tolerated his failing performance in bed, but he was not sure she would do that forever. She was still a looker, and other men would want her to warm the twilight of their lives. He should see a doctor, but somehow he was just too embarrassed. Online porn now gave him the thrill he needed, but he had to keep the laptop away from Pattie in case she checked up on him. He had an idea that there were some things that Pattie would not tolerate, and the casual browsing of sexy schoolgirls would likely be one of them. Some of the 'schoolgirls' should have graduated a long time ago; they looked a bit worn.

After a couple of hours' rehearsals, they went home to nap before the evening's gig, with Mick dropping Mak home and shouting conversation over the engine noise. He supposed Mick could hear his drums, but he was not sure he could hear much else.

Pattie and Mak returned to The Leopard at seven o'clock. Pattie had a new black dress and boots. She had paid a visit to the more upmarket hairdresser in the town and her silvery blonde hair shimmered with health. Despite doing the accounts, an appointment at Dearests Dos was out of the question. She suspected that she would end up bald if she once trusted herself to Delia and her dreadful apprentice.

'You look lovely tonight,' Mak said in the car.

Pattie suspected the compliment was in lieu of a Christmas gift and given the recent events, she would not make too much fuss over the festivities. She would make Mak a nice lunch tomorrow, and they would have some good wine. Christmas Day would be quiet and peaceful, and there was little chance of Mak's kids calling around with a present for him unless they wanted something, and they knew Pattie would not provide them with a free meal.

As soon as they got to the pub, Mak disappeared to do a final check as the other band members arrived. Pattie's job was to sell t-shirts. The band had ordered rather more than they could sell back in the days when they had expected to be as big as The Rolling Stones. Now the boxes in the garage at Delia's place had dwindled to a few dozen. Soon that revenue stream would be gone, and the Rocky and the Rainbows T-shirts would be consigned to the tumble dryer of history. At five pound each, they were a historic bargain. She sold six before the gig began and then moved to a table in the main bar, with the boxes tucked underneath. If anyone wanted a t-shirt, they all knew who to ask. Pattie had done her bit for tonight. She settled down with a drink, while Mak fussed over the band, making sure they left their phones and keys in Pattie's care.

Marilyn arrived with her mum and the kids and waved to Pattie coldly. Marilyn had wanted Mak, and she was still annoyed that he chosen Pattie, and she was stuck with the far less attractive Peter. Peter was a naturally gifted guitarist. He made no effort; just wandered in, tuned his guitar, strummed a few chords, checked the height of his microphone and was ready to perform. He barely even looked at the set list. What-ever Mak played, he could follow along regardless of the key. Peter should have succeeded, or at least, had a career as a session player, instead of a plumber, but he either did not value his talent or he just did not care.

All the band had dressed up for the performance, black jeans and new black t-shirts; rock and roll uniforms. They had never favoured flamboyant styles of dress. Only Peter squashed his feet into his old, tooled leather cowboy boots. The others wore comfortable shoes; the night could be long and hard on the knees. Playing rock and roll beyond forty was not unusual these days, but it did not respect ageing joints.

Mak's son Joe wandered in and disappeared outside with his father. Joe thought Mak's music was crap, but secretly envied his father's skill as a guitarist. Mak was good and he would be good until the arthritis or something worse got him. Pattie wondered for a moment if he had come to say some-thing about Aunt Maud. When Mak returned, a relaxed smile on his face, it told her that father and son had shared a smoke in the carpark and Joe had got fifty pounds out of his Dad and would now disappear to a club of his own choice. She should check Mak's pockets tonight in case the police called around over the next few days. Mak could be careless with his stash.

The audience was already lining up their drinks to save queuing at the bar, and the tables were full of packets of crisps and pork scratchings. A true British diet of extra fat was favoured.

The set began briskly. Mak liked to vary the tempo to keep the audience alternatively on their feet dancing or sitting down to get their breath back and drinking more beers. They played mostly covers now, plus the two or three original songs that had appeared on their albums years ago. They kicked off with a cover version of Free's 'All Right Now'; everyone knew the words, so things were off to a good start. Pattie settled back with her drink and listened to Mak's voice; singing or speaking, it didn't matter. It was the voice that made her want to lie down beside him and whisper 'love me'. He was playing well tonight thanks to Joe's little Christmas gift.

The chair next to her scrapped against the floor, and she looked up to see Kit Colley sit down beside her with a pint in his hand.

'Evenin' all,' he said, grinning.

He was well dressed; sharp black suit and a skinny black tie, smart leather loafers.

'Sit down, why don't you?'

'Do you mind?'

'Free country. Be my guest.'

Then they were silent until Mak had finished his version of 'Hotel California' to a well-deserved applause.

'He still plays better than anyone around here.'

'Yes, he does,' said Pattie fondly. 'To what do I owe the pleasure of your company tonight?'

'Purely social. Although I came to tell you, off the record, mind you, that Aunt Maud's death was likely accidental.'

'Oh,' said Pattie.

Then, after a silence.

'She was an elderly lady who liked two or three glasses of wine in the evening. What were you expecting? A Mafia hit?'

KC smiled at her. Wow, she is really pretty, he thought, and a good ten to fifteen years older than me. Life is so unfair sometimes.

'I just thought you would like to know, that's all. Make it easier for Mak over Christmas. Did you find her cat, by the way?'

'I am afraid Mak won't give his Aunt another thought in a few weeks. They were not a close family. Which cat are you talking about?'

'Aunt Maud's cat. We figured that she must have been outside calling her cat. Couldn't think of another reason for her to be outside in the freezing cold at night.'

'No, said Pattie, slightly puzzled, 'no cat. She hated animals, or rather, they hated her.

'I must be wrong, then. Maybe heard a noise or looking at the stars, who knows?'

'Maud would have needed quite a few glasses of wine before she saw any stars.'

'May I get you a drink?'

'Well, seeing as you are the law and I am only allowed one more before I go on the mineral water, you can buy me a large white wine. And some crisps.'

'Cheese and Onion?' he asked, smiling at her.

'Correct. Your powers of deduction astound me.'

Grinning to himself, KC headed for the bar. Pattie smiled sadly to herself and wished for a moment that she had been younger and single. The band launched into a slower version of 'Run Rudolph Run' by Chuck Berry. Mak was enjoying himself tonight. She smiled encouragingly towards the stage. The crowd was larger than usual for a Saturday night. There were not many places to go on Christmas Eve that did not charge a small fortune for drinks and even more for food. The

Leopard was cheap. The landlord had done a good job, and the bar was comfortable and not too airless and noisy, but it still looked cheap.

How far we have fallen, thought Pattie, from the swish clubs of London and New York. Hope was draining out of their life like water down the sink. Soon there would not be much left of the sunlit days. Pattie had been with Mak for almost ten years now and each year there seemed to be less and less to look forward to. Mak was getting deeper into debt, and it was all she could do to keep a roof over their head and feed them.

KC returned with the wine, a large bottle of mineral water, several bags of crisps and another pint for himself.

'Thanks, KC, you certainly know how to wine and dine a girl.'

'My pleasure, Ma'am.'

He sat down again, and both watched the band perform their version of 'Rock Me Baby'. They were playing superbly, and Mak was as good as he had ever been. The guitar solos ached with a latent sexual charge.

'He's still got it,' KC remarked.

'Of course he has.'

Pattie was not sure they were talking about music anymore. There seemed to be a connection between them, a spark of something that was not constrained by their age difference. She noticed that KC had the same measured voice as Mak, although lighter and chirpier. He did not have Mak's sexy growl, but she thought one day he might acquire it.

'So where did you study, Pattie?'

No point in lying about her education as she usually did. He could check up on her.

'Leeds. Economics. Did my masters at Sheffield.'

KC looked at her in admiration.

'Wow. Put you down as bright, but that is special.'

'Aren't you going to ask what happened? Most people do.'

'What happened?'

'Mak happened.'

'Ah.'

They both concentrated on the band. Pattie knew exactly what KC was thinking. She thought about it too, every day of her life. Life was shit, but only she could do anything about it. She was tied to Mak and letting him go was not an option for her anymore.'

The band finished the first half of their set, and it was time for a break. The second half was all Christmas songs, lots of high-energy stuff; they would need a break and a plate of chips before they tackled it. Mak came over and sat down, wiping the sweat from his forehead. He nodded at KC and waited for him to explain why he was there.

'Great first-half, Mak. All the old sparkle is still there.'

Mak nodded again. He felt unsure of KC, and he was saying nothing until the detective explained why he was there.

'This is really a social visit, Mak, but checking how you are doing and so on. Wanted to let you know, off the record, that your Aunt's death is likely to be an accident.'

'Cos it was.' Mak growled

Pattie could see that the two men did not like each other. The balance of power was unusual; KC was police, but he was on Mak's territory. Mak thought there was a new sparkle in Pattie's eyes, and he didn't like it.

'What would you like, luv?' Pattie wanted to smooth things over.

'Get me a whisky and a sandwich. Ham and pickle. I'm going to lie down for ten minutes, so bring it to me, please.'

He stood up and nodded again to KC.

'Thanks for the message. Enjoy your evening.'

That meant 'piss off' in Mak's language. He crossed to the stairs and went up to the small room that the band used on gig nights. KC and Pattie exchanged a look, and she excused herself to fetch Mak's drink.

KC sat down and stared into his beer. He had no plans, and he was enjoying Pattie's company, although he was unsure if she was feeling the same. He had an idea that Mak saw him as a threat and wanted him to leave. He might just wait until the second half was underway and then bow out gracefully. He was not sure why he was here, anyway. He had no obligation to update them on Aunt Maud's death, but either something was not sitting right, or he was attracted to Pattie.

Pattie returned just as the landlord moved to the stage to draw the raffle. His overdressed wife was pulling the winning tickets out of a large wastepaper basket and handing them to him. For some reason, she was wearing a fascinator on her head with what looked like wasps hovering around her forehead. A sad accessory from a wedding that would otherwise languish in tissue and would never to be worn again.

'Mak okay? He looks tired. It has been a stressful week, his Aunt dying and all.'

Pattie wished she could have a real conversation with this intriguing man, but she did not want a row with Mak later. It was Christmas, after all.

'Mak is just fine, thank you. It was good of you to take the trouble to tell us. I expect you will let us know the date of the inquest.'

KC looked disappointed for a second, but realising that this was his cue to leave, he finished his beer.

'Unlikely that there will be an inquest. I think we can sign off as an accidental death and release the body for burial after the holidays. Nice talking to you. Merry Christmas.'

He smiled, turned quickly away and left before she could reply. Pattie slumped down in her chair and poured herself a glass of mineral water. She would order some potato wedges and make a night of it.

SUNDAY 25 DECEMBER

Christmas in Britain is arguably the most depressing day of the year. It starts all soft and silent with a few cars tearing up the streets. If the day is clear and bright, there will soon be the sounds of people walking. If it is cold and dark, as it usually is, then the streets are haunted by sullen people with their equally miserable dogs. The next forty-eight hours, sometimes longer, are spent in the company of a close family, and few can say they enjoy that experience. Those with children might make a happy start of it, but that soon gives way to moaning and squabbling and the drone of the TV.

Christmas in a milder, warm climate is a far happier experience. In this cold, bleak island, most people lay in their bed during the dark early morning and wish they could stay there and just ignore the whole pathetic ritual. People living alone are portrayed by the media as if they are unwanted or neglected when, in fact, they spend a quiet, peaceful day free of other people. The media shows us happy families and there is no such thing.

Pattie and Mak just lay in bed, both feeling exhausted. Soon, Pattie would get up, make some breakfast, and leave Mak to snore away until the afternoon. The show last night had been good. One of the best for a few months. Nevertheless, the band had missed their chance, and they all knew it. Even with new technology allowing them to record and market their own music, they no longer had the energy or the skills to do it. Four albums would be all they had to show for their life in the music business, and one of those was a complete dud. The Rainbows were now consigned to the cover band scrap heap of history.

Pattie got up quietly and made herself come coffee. She wondered why KC had come along last night. He was a music fan, sure, but it seemed unnecessary to spend his Christmas Eve in a dump like The Leopard just to give them a snippet of information. She wondered for a moment if she was the reason and then dismissed the idea. He was in his forties; she was nearly sixty. She had a man, a confused, often drunken, impotent man, and part of her loved him. The other part hated him for the wrecking her life.

The day passed quietly, and Mak had even bought Pattie some perfume, although she suspected it was fake. She gratefully kissed him, and they shared a comfortable day together. There was something about loving someone for a long time. When the passion is gone, then at least you don't have to keep explaining. You both know. Mak seemed extraordinarily tired and retired to bed early, leaving Pattie to watch a movie alone. She preferred it that way, and when she joined him, she snuggled close to his back and enjoyed his warmth.

———

THURSDAY 12 JANUARY

Two weeks passed, and there was an official police phone call to say that Aunt Maud's body could be released to the undertaker. Mak looked helplessly at her, so Pattie found the name of a local firm and called with instructions. She and Mak didn't know if his Aunt had any special wishes about her burial, but they thought cremation would be fine. The police allowed them into the house, and they went through the bureau in the front room until a dog-eared brown envelope full of documents was found. The name of the solicitor was inside. Mak called them up and made an appointment for the next day. Pattie was not sure if he had read the will and she did not press him.

'Who pays for all this?' he asked Pattie.

'Comes out of the estate, I think. Solicitor will tell you tomorrow.'

'I keep thinking about what she might have wanted,' said Mak sadly. 'Want to give her the best send-off I can.'

Pattie thought he looked terribly troubled, but all she could do was go with him and lend her support. She secretly hoped that he would get the house. That at least would take the pressure off his finances. The usual phone calls about late payments had come after Christmas, but she would manage to put them off with the news of his Aunt's sudden death.

Later that day, there was a call from Kit Colley to say the house keys were now with the solicitor. Pattie answered the phone.

'How was your Christmas?' he asked her.

'Quiet. Not much to celebrate.'

'No. How is Mak doing?'

'He is just fine. Thanks for asking.'

She put the phone down and turned to see Mak standing behind her. He looked unsteady, and she thought he might have already had a drink that day.

'Why does that guy keep ringing? Huh? He sweet on you or something?' Mak seemed rather angry.

'He just wanted to say the keys were delivered to the solicitor. He asked how you were.'

'Right then. Right. Well, he fucking well needs to leave you alone.'

'Can't stand the competition, Mak?'

She knew she was provoking him, but he was unreasonable.

Mak stood very still, and for a moment, Pattie wondered if he wanted to hit her. They looked at each other, both angry, then Mak turned and retreated, slamming the bedroom door.

'What the hell is wrong with you, Mak?'

He didn't hear her. She wondered that if she had been closer, he would have slapped her. If he had, it would be the first and last time. She was sure of that.

The next morning, they drove to the solicitor's office. It was modern and plastic but still had that air of dust accumulating over the centuries. The young solicitor, who was well dusted, came out of her office to meet them, her high heels clicking on the wooden floor. Ms Katya Nowak showed them in and asked them to sit while Mak's eyes followed her tight skirt around the desk.

'Thank you for coming in, Mr Mason and Ms?'

'Harding,' said Pattie. 'I am Mak's partner, have been for ten years.'

Pattie had wanted that fact on the record before they got to the question of Mak's ex-wife.

'Ms. Harding,' she nodded. 'Nice of you both to come. I expect you have realised, Mr Mason, that your Aunt, Mrs Maud Betts, has made you the sole beneficiary. You inherit the house and a small sum of money, which should be adequate to cover the funeral expenses. I will arrange for you to have access to it quickly. A Grant of Probate normally comes through in about six weeks, and I see no complications in this case.'

'So how soon can I sell the house?' Mak asked.

'I would suggest,' said the solicitor gently, 'that you arrange for the house to be cleared. You can take any items of sentimental value and then you can arrange for a professional to clear the house. They will usually take most things and may even give you some money if the furniture is worth anything. It is the least stressful way of proceeding.'

She was looking at Mak as if she was dealing with someone still grieving for his relative. Clearly, it was her standard bedside manner for bereaved relatives and attractive older men.

'You can instruct an estate agent to do a valuation with a view to selling and they might like to take some photos while the house is still furnished. It looks better in the brochure.'

Pattie wondered, and not for the first time, if all the local businesses conspired to help each other. She would not be surprised if they did.

'Now there is the question of Mrs Mason.'

Mak looked confused.

'Your wife, Mrs Delia Mason.'

'Ex-wife,' said Mak firmly. 'She threw me out ten years ago.'

'I believe she lives in a property that you own, and you have been separated for ten years. The property is not jointly owned, I understand?'

'She's called, hasn't she?' Mak snapped. 'Money grabbing bitch, she is not getting a penny.'

'There is no reason that she should, Mr Mason. In answer to your question, Mrs Delia Mason has called me, and I was unable to give her any information, as she is not named in the will. I simply asked because I want to establish your intentions.'

Mak calmed down and replied.

'I want to sell Aunt Maud's house and pay off the rest of the mortgage on Delia's house. Then my overdraft and credit cards, then some of the mortgage on the kid's house, maybe sell that one too. That's my thinking.'

'And do you plan to keep the house or hand it over to your ex-wife as a divorce settlement?'

'Give her the house?'

Mak had not considered this. He could hand over the house and be free of Delia. He thought for a minute.

'I really do not see why Dearest should be handed a house when she has not contributed a penny, and she owns a business. I have been gone for ten years; the kids are grown up. I don't owe her anything.'

This was fighting talk from Mak and Pattie was pleased. He might finally do something about Delia and the parasite children.

'My advice, Mr Mason, is to sell your Aunt's property and pay off the mortgage on the house that your wife is living in. The marriage ended some time ago, and you can quite legally put that house up for sale, too. If you start divorce proceedings, and this is simple as you have been separated for over two years, it is likely your wife will put in a claim for fifty percent of that property and may, given her circumstances, want to buy your share and continue to live there.'

Delia had not ingratiated herself with Ms Nowak after making a rather aggressive phone call demanding information about the will. But Mak was her client, and she could see that acting on his behalf would ensure the firm got his business when he sold the houses.

'Well,' Mak said slowly, 'I think I might take your advice. If I wanted to sell the kid's house, we could do that too.'

'Why yes, but I think you might want to delay that and talk to your children first. It could be that they have future plans and it would be kinder to discuss it before we act.'

'And you would tell, Dearest?' Mak asked tentatively.

Pattie thought, what a coward he is. He has found a way to avoid telling Delia himself. She expected the screaming row that would follow might require her to referee.

'I suggest, Mr Mason, that I write to Mrs Mason and tell her formally that you are the sole heir to your Aunt's property. At the same time, inform her that you have directed me to start divorce proceedings prior to the sale of the family house and to advise her, she will receive fifty percent from the proceeds of that sale. It is what the court would likely award her, and it will give her time to arrange funds if she wants to buy your half.'

Mak looked relieved. She was solving his problems for him. He was already half in love with her.

'I would also suggest that if your Aunt has any valuable jewellery or things that you make a gift to your wife. To sweeten the pill.'

Katya Nowak was clever. Wheeling and dealing was what she did best, and her pretty face and neat curves helped her do it well. Pattie felt, on the one hand, relieved and on the other, sickened by Mak's leering at the young woman. Sometimes Mak disgusted her, even though it was his charm and a flirtatious way that had first won her heart. However, those were different days. Some men, and Mak was one of them, had no idea that things were different now.

It was agreed, and Ms Nowak said she would arrange to contact the undertaker so all the bills could be settled out of the estate.

'And when is the letter likely to be sent to Mrs Mason?' Pattie asked, speaking for the first time since entering the office. 'I want to be sure to be out of town when it arrives.'

She grinned at Mak, knowing he had other ideas. She had no plans to bear the sharp, pointy end of Delia's rage, but she feared that she would.

'I will call and tell you. It should be about ten days,' said Ms Nowak, warmly shaking Mak's hand as they left.

———

TUESDAY 17 JANUARY

There is no such thing as a good day for a funeral. If it is warm and sunny, the living feel guilty. If it is wet and cold, then it reflects the mood of the mourners and seems more appropriate, but it depresses everyone. The day of Aunt Maud's funeral was unexpectedly bright but extremely cold. The streets were bleak, and most people had taken down their overblown Christmas lights. With Christmas over, all the optimism was draining from the country and with Brexit looming, there was not much to celebrate. The mourners had not counted on such a sunny day and tried to maintain a somber mood in the face of the winter sunshine.

Aunt Maud had left no specific instructions, so Mak has opted for the basic cremation with no frills. This was in case he had to pay up front. Luckily, the accommodating Katya Nowak had arranged for the estate to foot the bill. Pattie has chosen the flowers and Mak chose two popular songs from the forties that he thought his Aunt might like.

It seemed Aunt Maud had a lot of friends locally, although it was hard to tell if they were real friends or just nosy-parkers tagging along. Delia arrived dramatically supported by Janis. She was wearing a black coat with a huge fur collar and looked the part of the grieving relative. Pattie wore a warm blue checked coat and had convinced Mak to wear a suit under his long leather coat. The coat was shabby, but he was warm. She was concerned about Mak's health right now; he seemed withdrawn and edgy, not himself. Joe turned up in jeans, a baseball cap and bright green gloves. He looked cold and embarrassed.

The hearse arrived, and the assembled company stubbed out their cigarettes and trooped into the crematorium. The celebrant, who certainly had never known Aunt Maud, gave a brief biography of her life. A few eyebrows raised when they learnt she drove a bus during the war.

'Well done, Auntie Maud.' Pattie muttered to Mak and squeezed his hand. Mak smiled sadly.

The plush curtains closed on the coffin to the strains of Rosemary Clooney singing 'Blues in the Night', and everyone filed out after a moment's solemn reflection. They all stood uncomfortably in the entrance, waiting to find out if a slap-up lunch was on the cards. They were disappointed when Mak announced that he was going to the pub and hoped others might join him to toast his Aunt. Everyone knew that Mak would not be buying the drinks and most drove off home to get out of the cold. Mak and Pattie, with Delia, Janis and a couple of neighbours went to the pub at the end of Maud's street. Mak stood a round of drinks, first having borrowed the money from Pattie, and everyone sat silently, as no one seemed to want to talk much.

'I quite like funerals,' said Delia.

'Stop it, Mum,' Janis protested.

'Well, we all have to go sometime,' Delia said irritatingly. 'Poor Aunt Maud, dying that way. What a shock it was finding her like that.'

'Sure, you told us before, Dearest,' snapped Mak.

'I am just saying it was a shock, that's all.'

There was a lull, and everyone stared into their drinks, most hoping that Mak would pay for another round. Mak sat huddled in his coat with his hands in his pockets. He was quiet and tetchy as he had been since the death. Pattie had found him at least once this week, with all his bills laid out on the kitchen table and a pad of pencil jottings. When she offered to help, he snapped at her.

'Just because you got a degree in economics, you think you are bloody clever, don't you? You always looked down on me, Pattie, like I'm an idiot. Always.'

There was no sense in answering; reasoning with him. Later, she heard him shut in the bathroom with both taps running. Mak was sobbing. The best she could do now their sex life had become a farce was to cuddle up to him at night and share her warmth.

The next morning, Mak went to his Aunt's house alone to show the estate agents around and let them take photographs. Then he arranged for the clearance. That day he came home with some boxes containing jewellery, photographs and family documents. He also brought a new television from the bedroom and the new toaster from Argos, which stayed on the hall table, box lid flapping, until Pattie put it in the cupboard.

On Wednesday morning, Katya Nowak called to say that the letter to Delia would go by post that day. Pattie took the call, and as Mak was in the bedroom finishing his set list for the bingo that afternoon, she did not trouble him with the news. She calculated that it would arrive on Friday lunchtime and they would be safely at the bingo club when Delia opened it. She would suggest that they went into town to eat after the set. She could invent some shopping that had to be collected. That way, they would be out of Delia's reach until Sunday as she was unlikely to lose money on her busiest day in the salon just to come over and shout at Mak.

———

FRIDAY 20 JANUARY

F riday morning passed without interruption, and once they were at the bingo club, Pattie deliberately turned off Mak's phone, which he put in her handbag. It seemed likely that the solicitor's letter would arrive late morning and maybe Delia would not see it until the evening. The set started well.

Good afternoon everybody and welcome to Friday's with Mak and Happy Friday and welcome to everyone out there on Long Time Radio. You can tune in 24/7 on longtimeradio.com. You all know how to do it. I got a load of music lined up for the next couple of hours and hopefully, you'll like some of them; hopefully, you'll like all of them. But, if you don't and you have particular tunes that you desperately want to hear, give my lovely Pattie a shout, and I'll do whatever I can. In the meantime, here's Ed Sheeran with the fabulous tune from the TV series Sons of Anarchy. This is 'Make It Rain'.

Pattie settled down to enjoy the set. Mak knew how to pick the songs, and he knew how to sell them to his audience. This song was a favourite of hers, even though she had never seen the TV series. Mak thought Ed Sheeran had real talent and bought most of his albums. This was a departure, as he tended to disparage current musical styles in favour of his own era. She wondered about Mak. Was it love, or dependence that kept them together now? She had an idea that there was a point in a relationship where these became the same thing.

When they had first met, Pattie worked for the record company, running several accounts and progressing rapidly up the company hierarchy. Then Mak walked into her office, and all that ended. He was tall and good looking, with a funny smile; a rising star. The original five-piece band was going places. Then they were down to four with their vocalist dead in a pool of booze and vomit in a hotel room after the US tour. Mak took over his role, and they struggled on for a few more years until the band members went back to being plumbers, builders and a librarian. Mak took on the DJ gigs to make ends meet.

She had never entirely worked out what the attraction was, but the sex was amazing for a lot of years. Now here they were in a provincial town, living from one week to the next on what they clawed together. The rise to rock and roll stardom was all fair-weather friends and fireworks, but the road down was burgers and launderettes. Only the alcohol travelled both roads.

So Christmas holidays are all over, and I hope you had a really brilliant time with too much of everything. Now it is back on the diets for you all. So, to keep you all fairly chilled out and relaxed is a little tune called, 'Blues on Holiday'. And this is the amazing Susan Tedeschi.

. . .

A few people wandered onto the minuscule dance floor in front of the stage, but most were content to sit still. In most cases, the extra weight their Christmas feeding frenzy had added would take many months to shed. Over Christmas, there was no incentive to do much other than eat and watch TV. Mak was an expert at sensing their moods and finding the music to complement it. Then, with a loud crash, the street door swung open abruptly, and the cold rushed in. People looked over, scowling at the inconsiderate intruder, as Delia flounced in, boot heels thumping on the floor. Mak looked up from the stage and knew exactly why she had come.

'You bastard,' she screamed at Mak over the music.

'Do you know what he's have done? Can you imagine what he's done?'

She was addressing the whole club, waving her arms and wrongly assuming that they cared about her problems other than for the gossip it provided.

'And don't you sit there looking smug.' She had just spotted Pattie.

'You wanted my husband from the very first. Didn't care that he left me with two kids to raise on me own. You didn't care what happened to us, did you, you fucking cow?'

The audience was enjoying this. Pattie knew that she could not respond. It was all true. Although Delia did forget to mention the fact that she threw Mak out when she found out about his affair with Pattie. She got the house, and the kids were both fed. Mak was just not there anymore. So far, Delia had not moved any closer to either Mak or Pattie. She remained centre stage. She had an audience, and they were going to hear it all.

'And now, and can you believe this, he is divorcing me and selling my house out from under me after all these years of marriage and all my hard work raising his kids and building my business, while he swanned around with that no-good tart over there, who thinks she is better than the rest of us. Can you believe it? You bastard, Mak.'

She stopped for breath, and the club waited for a reaction.

A rather drunken voice from the back of the room shouted.

'Yo Mak! Well done, mate. Now you can marry Pattie, and we can all get pissed at your wedding.'

He stood up, raising his glass in a toast. The rest of the club laughed, and Mak quickly put on another louder, more up-tempo song without making an introduction.

Delia stood furiously clutching her phone and her car keys, and for a moment, it looked like she might throw them at Mak. Then the strains of 'Nutbush City Limits' lured a few women out to do the line dance that was popularised by the song. The bingo caller, sensing it was time to eject Delia, went over and took her arm.

'Now calm down, Dearest, luv. I don't want to get nasty, but I think it is time for you to go home, don't you?'

'Don't call me luv, you prick,' snarled Delia, pushing his hand off her and addressing Mak again. 'I am going but Mak, you gonna be hearing from my lawyers. Do you understand? I am fighting this, do you hear? You can't divorce me after all the years I've given you. This is shit, and I'm fighting it.'

She was wasting her time. Too much information. They were not listening to her anymore and Delia, realising that she may have overreacted, returned to her salon and a more sympathetic audience. Mak looked relieved, and a few men came over to Pattie with requests for songs and to give her a hug. Any excuse to feel my tits, thought Pattie.

'You are a champion, Pattie,' one of them said. 'Don't you take any notice of that sour old bag. You're a real lady.'

Pattie felt soiled.

———

SUNDAY 29 JANUARY

Mak had a special place he liked to go when he needed to think. In the middle of the town, which was so remote from the sea that fish was a luxury, was a garden of knots. Enormous knots, the sort that sailors tied in days gone by. They were made from iron and stood like stick figures over six feet tall. Some were wide, like giant bundles of wire knitting wool. The garden had been there since the days of the promised regeneration of the town, and now the few remaining benches were home to old men with nowhere else to go. Fish and chip papers overflowed from the bins and the pigeons feasted daily on the scraps of human greed.

Mak liked it because it was quiet and it was away from the flat. Not that Pattie didn't allow him space and privacy. She was the least intrusive person he knew. She didn't crowd him, and when he closed a door, she knocked rather that bursting in on his peace. It was her way of showing respect; her way of saying we are two separate people. He loved her for it.

He was still with Delia when he first met Pattie. The marriage was disintegrating and was coming to an end. The lack of love on both sides was evident and the children, Janis, named for Janis Joplin, and Joe, so called because they both liked the name, were almost teenagers. Mak had enjoyed family life when they were little. He brought them presents and rushed home to be with them after a spell on the road. Delia, who knew the score when she married him, was becoming increasingly fed up with Mak's unconventional life-style. The band had recorded their third album, and things were going well. But the troupes of fans and groupies were getting on Delia's nerves, and she was less and less tolerant, although she knew that after most gigs the band was too drunk or too stoned to do much other than throw up, then fall asleep.

At first, his dealings with Pattie were strictly professional. She looked after their account and provided day-to-day oper-ating funds. He looked at her, of course. She was pretty, with a mane of blonde hair that he thought might be natural, and a cute habit of standing twirling on one stiletto heel with her hand on her desk for balance. If the light was right, then her hair lit up like it was a halo. She wore black; it was her uniform. One day, Mak asked her if she would like to have dinner with him. She weighed up the offer, but as it was general knowledge that Mak's marriage was at an end, she said yes.

That evening was magical. They locked eyes across the dinner table, and the spark turned into a flame. They shared their life stories over a bottle of wine and then went back to Pattie's flat and rolled into each other's arms and laughed while they made love. The next morning, they shared break-fast and then went on their way. Pattie went to the office and Mak to a recording session. That day he played liked he was inspired; every note was pure and accurate.

For the next two weeks, he was away doing gigs and fielding the daily round of intrusive phone calls from Delia. The kids needed this; kids needed that. Being in any sort of relationship seemed like a curb to his freedom. Women tied you down, he thought. Trading Delia for Pattie was beginning to seem like a bad idea. He didn't stop for one moment to consider what Pattie might want. In his mind, she was a woman, and she would want the same things that Delia wanted, and it would drain him. After a few days, he convinced himself that he didn't want a relationship with Pattie. The next hurdle was plucking up the courage to tell her. He thought whatever he said would upset her and kept putting it off. When he finally did, he got a reaction that stunned him.

He went to her office with his prepared speech about how she was a wonderful woman, but that it had been a bad idea to sleep together. Behind his back, he had a bunch of pink roses as a peace offering. Pink seemed an acceptable colour for break-up flowers. He said he really could not sustain another relationship. He had been trying to find a way to tell her without upsetting her. He was sorry. He waited for the tears and protestations, but neither came. Instead, Pattie stood up and balancing on one heel as she habitually did. She told him very quietly what she thought of him.

'How dare you come in here now and say this to me? You despicable, pathetic coward. What gives you the right to assume I want a relationship with you? I cannot believe that you of all people are still seeing women in this ridiculous old-fashioned way. I have a career, my own money, my own life. How dare you presume that after one night that I want a 'relationship', as you call it? Maybe I regarded you as a casual fuck, in the same way as you seem to have regarded me. How dare you come in here and patronise me?'

Mak took a step back. He had seen plenty of angry women, but not like this. There was not a high petulant whine, just a low, steady growl of real fury. He thought he should leave when she took a step towards him, and he flinched.

'You know what makes me so angry apart from your outdated, chauvinistic idea of a relationship? You are robbing me of your friendship.'

She stopped and glared at him.

'I valued our friendship. It was important to me. More important that one night in bed. I liked you; I enjoyed your company. I called you a friend. Now you are taking that away from me, like a spoilt child in the playground. How dare you?'

There were no tears, no screaming, just anger. Mak was unsure what to say. He produced the roses from behind his back and held them out to her, mouthing 'I'm sorry'. Pattie took the bunch and considered them. They were beautiful, fragrant; a dozen long stemmed pink roses tied with a ribbon. They had cost Mak the best part of ten pounds. Then slowly and with complete control, she broke the roses in half over her knee and threw them at him. Then she spun on her heel and turned back to her desk, sat down and continued with her work. Mak had no idea what to say. He stood for a moment, waiting for her to speak, but she ignored him. Embarrassed, he stooped and picked up the shattered bouquet and left. He quickly dumped the roses in the nearest bin.

Now, ten years later, as he sat alone in the cold steel and concrete wasteland, he realised that he had to solve his financial problems. If he didn't, Pattie would leave, and that terrified him. Mak sat watching the sun glint on the huge sculptures until he started to feel the cold. So far, Delia had kept her distance after her ill-timed outburst in the bingo club. He knew she would be angry, but it was time to break all the ties. Soon he would have the money to pay off the first of the mortgages.

Now it was time to face his kids. He felt guilty for leaving them with their mother. He figured it was better for him to leave than have them grow up in the war zone that life with Delia had become. He did once suggest to Pattie that maybe they could visit or stay with them. Pattie just said firmly, 'Your kids, you visit them. I want absolutely no part of this.'

He knew that she meant it and the subject never arose again. He took them out to the cinema, to concerts when they were teenagers, but somehow there was no real connection. They both had Delia's image stamped on them. He saw to it that they had everything they needed.

They had moved into his second house, his investment property, as they got older and when life with Delia got too awful for them. Some investment. They never paid rent and came to him when things broke down. Pattie put a stop to the requests for money and anyway, he didn't have any. His record royalties were dwindling, and he was very aware that for the last five years, Pattie had paid most of the bills.

He felt he had been more than fair to Delia. If she wanted to buy him out and keep her house, he'd offered to take twenty thousand less that the market value. Now he was planning to sell the kid's house, and he didn't suppose either could buy it. Janis helped her mother in the salon and had her own nail business where she went to your home and did a manicure. There had been an idea to put the nail salon in with the hair salon. Call it Dearest & Daughter. Health and safety put pay to that when the ventilation in the salon was deemed barely adequate for public use, let alone handle the toxic acetone fumes.

Mak had no idea what his son Joe did for a living. Mak had given him a guitar as soon as he was big enough to hold one, but somehow the music was not in his veins. Then he went to Art College with few visible results. Now he seemed to do nothing all day. He occasionally showed up at the Leopard and sold Mak a bag of weed before the show. He usually hung around and smoked some of it, too. There would be trouble if Pattie ever found out.

He wrapped his leather coat closely around him and started for the other side of the town and the row of terraced houses where Janis and Joe lived. It was Sunday morning, so they were likely to be home. The salon was closed that day, so unless Janis were out with her mother, she would be there.

Joe, as far as he knew, never went anywhere during daylight hours. Like a vampire.

Mak didn't like walking much but parking his car close to the kid's house was pretty much impossible on a Sunday morning. The terraced streets were lined with vehicles, car after car, all in the same poor condition, with peeling paintwork and amateur botched repairs. People around here were poor, but they all had a car and a big TV, even if they could not afford them. Somehow, they were deemed as necessary.

He knocked on the door and waited for his daughter to appear in her fleecy dressing gown. She let him in and wandered through to the kitchen and put the kettle on for coffee. Once the water was boiled, she plonked a cup of instant coffee in front of Mak and went back to her iPad. Occasionally she smiled or muttered to herself, as if faces on the iPad might talk back. After a long time, Mak took his coffee and went through to the lounge and put the gas fire on. He sat on the edge of the sofa and looked around the very untidy room. He cleared the piles of clothes and magazines from the sofa, took his shoes off and settled down to wait for his daughter to finish whatever it was she was doing. Eventually, he dozed off and was woken by Joe, who was looking for a cigarette in the jackets hung over the chairs.

'Morning Joe.'

There was no answer. Joe nodded to his Dad, and Mak could see the headphones. Joe was enjoying his music and Mak hoped it was the right kind but was pretty sure it was not. Joe found the squashed packet of cigarettes that he was looking for and disappeared into the kitchen. His memory lasted from twelve till noon on a good day. The house was quiet, and the room was warm. Mak thought that perhaps a world full of people wearing headsets would be pleasantly quiet. Everyone would hear different music. No wonder everything seemed so disconnected; no one shared the same songs anymore.

After a couple of hours, Mak woke. The house was silent.

He looked into the kitchen. His children were sitting on either side of the table. Janis was still on her iPad, and Joe was drinking coffee and smoking. Mak made himself another coffee and then went back to the warm room and put the TV on. He found an old Western playing on catch-up TV and settled down to wait for his kids to return to earth. He saw most of the movie between naps and when it ended, he was hungry. We went back to the kitchen to find the tableau still in place.

'Anyone hungry?'

Janis looked up and nodded. She pointed to the fridge and the magnet on the door, which Mak fetched and handed over to his daughter.

'Mine is Margherita with extra cheese,' said Mak, hoping he would not have to pay for this meal.

Janis placed an order online, then went back to her Facebook page. Mak concluded that this was a regular way of ordering food and it was probably all they ate. He washed up the cups and cleared the table while they waited for the food. When they had been young, he tried to stop them from eating junk food. He told them that happy meals were made from the baby animals when they got too big for the children's zoo. It worked for a while.

Sooner or later, the kids would be ready for a conversation. He wondered if they were like this all the time, each locked in their personal electronic world. Did they ever talk to each other?

Finally, the doorbell rang, and Janis went to answer it. Mak found three beers in the fridge and placed them on the table. The pizzas were placed in the centre of the table, and Janis cut them up with a special knife that looked like a weapon of torture from a Kung Fu movie. She handed each a large piece of kitchen towel, and they dined in silence. No plates, no cutlery, no glasses, and no napkins. Just boxes of pizza, bottles of beer and paper towels. What ever happened to fine dining, thought Mak? We are living in the world without washing up.

At the end of the meal, Mak sensed that this was his moment. He reached over and took the iPad from Janis and indicated to his son to take off his headset. Joe screwed his face up and untangled the headset from his hair. A strange strangled sound faintly played in the background. Mak looked at his son and waited until the sounds stopped.

'Now listen up, you two. I have something important to say. This is the plan, and there are to be no arguments. Got it? I am putting both houses on the market.'

Two pairs of eyes suddenly looked at him in alarm.

'I am giving your Mother, half of the family house, which she is entitled to and will sell her my half if she wants it. I am also divorcing her, which I should have done years ago. I am selling this house, and you two will have to organise where you will live and start paying your way.'

Janis opened her mouth to protest.

'So no arguments. The decision is final. Once everything is sold, Pattie and I are leaving. So, thanks for the delightful lunch, guys. I will let you know when the estate agent is coming round.'

He collected his coat from the hall and went out into the cold afternoon air.

———

TUESDAY 31 JANUARY

Tuesday rolled around, and after a day of frantic calls between Delia and Janis, they agreed to meet at Delia's house on that evening for a conference. Joe was not convinced at first and said he was busy, to which Janis replied, 'Crap, you never do anything anyway'. Another phone call to her mother got the promise of food, and so Joe lethargically agreed to be there.

Delia left the salon early and took a trip to Tescos to get a ready-to-eat barbecued chicken and some bottles of beer. When Janis and Joe arrived, she heated some oven chips and tinned peas. Joe wandered around the kitchen until he found the beer, helped himself and then slouched by the sink waiting for his food. The three settled around the kitchen table to eat and vent their anger towards Mak, and by association, Pattie.

'She has ruined him,' said Delia.

Having got that off her chest, she moved on to how dreadful it was after all these years that she should be divorced against her will.

'Don't be a pain, Mum', Janis complained, 'Divorce him and get your share. You never know who might come along once people know you are single again.'

'But it is so hurtful,' wailed Delia, as Joe took both the chicken legs and ate them with his fingers.

Janis waited for her mother to settle down again.

'Look, Mum, he has offered you his half of this house, for twenty thou less than the valuation, right?'

Delia nodded as she sniffed.

'So you have savings, and you have a business, why not go get a mortgage and buy him out. Get a second valuation of your own to check his figures, and then go see the building society. This house is worth about three hundred and fifty, right? That means you are going to get his share for around a hundred and fifty. You can't buy a slum terrace for that these days.'

She waited as Delia had some more chips and thought about it.

'Joe, what do you think?'

Joe was finishing the second leg and was thinking about a cute blonde with an interesting tattoo he met on the weekend and whether she might sleep with him later that week. He grunted at his sister.

Taking this as agreement, Janis waited for her Mother to download the idea.

The plates were cleared, and a bright green Violetta was produced from the fridge and divided into three. A generous dollop cream was added to each bowl, and the family ate in silence for five minutes.

Once dessert was eaten, Delia was ready to consider the options.

'Okay, so I buy Mak out and put up with that bitch forcing him to divorce me. What else will I get? Do I get a share of your place when he sells it? And some cash?'

'I suppose you could ask,' said Janis tentatively. 'No harm in trying is there. But what about me and Joe, Mum?'

Tuesday rolled around, and after a day of frantic calls between Delia and Janis, they agreed to meet at Delia's house on that evening for a conference. Joe was not convinced at first and said he was busy, to which Janis replied, 'Crap, you never do anything anyway'. Another phone call to her mother got the promise of food, and so Joe lethargically agreed to be there.

Delia left the salon early and took a trip to Tesco's getting a ready-to-eat barbecued chicken and some bottles of beer. When Janis and Joe arrived, she heated some oven chips and tinned peas. Joe wandered around the kitchen until he found the beer, helped himself and then slouched by the sink, waiting for his food. The three settled around the kitchen table to eat and vent their anger towards Mak, and by association, Pattie.

'She has ruined him,' said Delia.

Having got that off her chest, she moved on to how dreadful it was after all these years that she should be divorced against her will.

'Don't be a pain, Mum,' Janis complained. 'Divorce him and get your share. You never know who might come along once people know you are single again.'

'But it is so hurtful,' wailed Delia, as Joe took both the chicken legs and ate them with his fingers.

Janis waited for her mother to settle down again.

'Look, Mum, he has offered you his half of this house, for twenty thou less than the valuation, right?'

Delia nodded as she sniffed.

'So you have savings, and you have a business. Why not go get a mortgage and buy him out? Get a second valuation of your own to check his figures and then go see the building society. This house is worth about three hundred and fifty, right? That means you are going to get his share for around a hundred and fifty. You can't buy a slum terrace for that these days.'

She waited, as Delia had some more chips and thought about it.

'Joe, what do you think?'

Joe was finishing the second leg and was thinking about a

cute blonde with an interesting tattoo he met on the weekend and whether she might sleep with him later that week. He grunted at his sister.

Taking this as agreement, Janis waited for her Mother to download the idea.

The plates were cleared, and a bright green Violetta was produced from the fridge and divided into three. A generous dollop of cream was added to each bowl, and the family ate in silence for five minutes.

Once dessert was eaten, Delia was ready to consider the options.

'Okay, so I buy Mak out and put up with that bitch, forcing him to divorce me. What else will I get? Do I get a share of your place when he sells it? And some cash?'

'I suppose you could ask,' said Janis tentatively. 'No harm in trying, is there? But what about me and Joe, Mum?'

Janis was hoping her Mum would be sensible about things and so cleared the plates to the dishwasher and started to make tea for everyone. It was time to show what a model daughter she was.

'I'm getting a place in Manchester,' Joe said, in case anyone was interested. 'I know a bloke with a squat in the city.'

'Right, dear, that's a good idea.'

Delia would be glad to be free of her son. He would never amount too much; he borrowed money, and he ate a lot of food. He was just like Mak. Janis was different.

'So Janis,' she said speculatively. 'When your house is sold, I thought you might want to live here with me. We could fix up the front room, and you could do your nails from home and pay a bit of rent.'

This was exactly what Janis had in mind; except for the bit of rent, which she could probably get out of.

Joe, having eaten all that was on offer, said he had to go and taking another beer for the road, he left to go home and watch TV. He had ideas for his future, but they did not include his mother or his sister.

Delia and Janis spend a friendly evening watching Poldark and discussing the hairstyles.

'Don't she look a mess? Didn't they have combs back then?'

Janis stayed the night, thinking it might be time to sort out her room at her Mum's place. She did not plan to clear up the other house before it went up for sale. Best to move now and leave it to Joe. Joe, of course, was thinking the same thing and was planning to drop over to Manchester when his dole money arrived. Assuming all was now settled, she would go with Delia to see the solicitor and then call her Dad to tell him what she had arranged. Delia was quite capable of changing her mind at this stage and needed a close watch. Convincing her to buy Mak's half of the house was the simple part; it was the divorce that was needling Delia. No amount of careful explanation would convince her mother that the divorce was inevitable. They separated ten years ago, so it would happen whether she wanted it or not. If she caused a fuss, there was a chance that Mak would withdraw his offer of the favourable deal on the house, or even make her fight for her share. That would be costly, and Janis was already future proofing her share in the family home.

––––––

WEDNESDAY 1 FEBRUARY

The next day, mother and daughter dressed up smart and then went to the salon to fix their hair while Paulina went for take-away coffees and muffins. After this comforting start to their day, they left Paulina in charge of the early appointments, as Delia and Janis walked through the shopping centre on a distracting route to the solicitors. It was warm inside and enticing, and some garments were earmarked to try on during the return journey. Janis watched her mother carefully but did not discuss the previous evening's resolutions. It was important not to add new ideas to the carefully worked out plan. Just outside the centre, as they crossed to the solicitor's office in the market square, a customer greeted them.

'Hello, Mrs Mason, so sorry about your Aunt. Must have been such a shock for you. How are you bearing up?'

Delia said she was bearing up nicely, thank you.

'There must be so much to arrange after a sudden death. I know when my husband had his stroke and died, I was in and out of that office (she nodded towards the solicitor's office) every day. It went on for weeks; I could tell you some stories.'

Janis took a step forward in the hope that she would not start on the stories.

'Well, I won't detain you, luv. Give my sympathies to your lovely husband.'

She giggled, remembering who knows what about Mak and waddled on her way, shopping bags at the ready.

The damage was done. Janis could see the change of heart written on her mother's face as soon as they arrived at the overheated reception. All she could do now was to try to steer her mother back on course with the help of Mr Arnold, the solicitor. They were shown into his office, which had been his father's and his grandfather's office before him. The disappointing birth of his only child, a daughter, made it feel like the end of the family line. He was having trouble imagining little Rhiannon making it to law school. Now he had to spend thirty minutes with Mrs Mason, who had a perfectly intelligent son, who did nothing all day.

'So', he began. 'What have you decided? Shall we be sensible and take your husband's offer of the reduced purchase price? I can make a couple of calls to colleagues for you and start the ball rolling towards a mortgage.'

Delia sensed she was being patronised. It was the principal here, she felt. She must stand up to Mak for once. He could not always have what he wanted, and she did not want a divorce. She was Mrs Makenzie Mason; she did not want things to change.

'No, Mr Arnold, we will not be sensible, as you call it. We will fight. I do not want a divorce. I want to keep my house, and he can keep the kid's house. I think that is fairer, don't you?'

Mr Arnold looked wearily at Janis, who shrugged her shoulders. The explanations began again.

'Mrs Mason, as I explained to you on the phone. You cannot contest this divorce. You have been separated for over ten years. He has a new partner, and she will have an equal claim now to any property acquired during their relationship.

If you go to court, it will be expensive, and the most you can expect is an equal share in the family home. We could try for part of the proceeds of the second house, but as he bought it after you separated, it is unlikely you will get anything, and the fees will be enormous. Be sensible here, Mrs Mason, accept his offer and buy him out and keep your house.'

Janis looked closely at her mother. She could not see the pain and shame of losing a husband she had thought was hers for life. Delia would lose the man who came running when she needed a plumber, or the washer broke down. He was a fixture in her life, and she did not want to lose him. Janis saw only an absent father who seemed to care little for any of them. She dimly remembered the fights and the dramas when they were small and how much better life had been when Mak moved out permanently.

Delia was firmly on her high horse now.

'No, Mr Arnold, we will fight this. Those are my instruction. I want my house, and he can keep the other one, but I will not agree to the divorce. And that woman he lives with is to get nothing.'

Mr Arnold gave up and accepted he was defeated. He was not looking forward to breaking the news to Delia when the divorce was granted without question, and the wrangling over the houses dragged on for months.

Having stated her terms, Delia returned to the salon feeling triumphant. Janis excused herself on the grounds of having to go to buy supplies from the chemist for her nail clients.

Delia's parting remark was, 'unless you get a wholesaler for those supplies you will never make a profit, my girl.'

'No, Mum,' said Janis, who was quite ready to slap her mother.

Janis headed for a warm cafe and had another muffin to help deal with the morning's setbacks. She should tell Mak that there was a problem. Surely, they could sort out the property and let the matter of the divorce go for a while. Divorced or not, it would make no difference to her mother in the end. But making sure that Delia got the house, and she moved in with her mother could make a huge difference to her future. She must try to get her father to agree to hold off on the divorce. She took out her phone and called her father's number.

As usual, Pattie answered.

'Mak's phone. You can leave a message with me.'

This was the standard response, whether it went to voice mail or not.

'Sorry to bother you, Pattie. Could I speak to Dad for a few minutes?'

Pattie stared at the phone, wondering what Janis wanted. Then she took the phone to Mak, who was getting ready for the afternoon's bingo.

'Your daughter.'

She held out the phone.

'My daughter?'

'Wake up, Mak,' said Pattie as she put the phone down on the table and walked out of the room.

'Hello.'

Mak was cautious. Daughter or not, she was as devious as her mother. Joe might be a waste of space, but he was honestly dishonest.

'Dad, I thought I should tell you that Mum won't accept the deal.'

Mak sighed loudly.

'Damn,' he hissed.' What does she want? Doesn't she realise that she can't stop me from divorcing her? She threw me out ten years ago, for Christ's sake.'

'And with good reasons, I believe,' said Janis sarcastically. 'Couldn't you settle the properties and hold off on the divorce? It makes no difference to you, does it? Not planning on marrying Pattie, are you?'

'Maybe. Maybe not. I should have married Pattie years ago if she would have me, but she won't.'

Mak was silent for a few minutes, and he was angry.

'Look, Janis, let me think about this, will you? I'll tell the solicitor when I decide what I am going to do. Until then, keep your nose out of my business and start looking for somewhere else to live. I'm bringing an estate agent round to your house. I still have keys, but just so you know, it will be on Saturday week, early. Make sure that place is not a shit heap, will you?'

He ended the call abruptly.

Janis thought she had heard something new in his voice. Something like tears of frustration mixed with a violent rage. She dismissed it. Parents were such a pain.

———

THURSDAY 9 FEBRUARY

Delia's change of heart left Mak feeling annoyed and frustrated. He knew she was stupid when he married her, but he married her anyway. In those days, she was much too pretty and sexy to allow her to fall into anyone else's hands or bed. But she was not a companion for life. She ran her business well; she had loyal clients and a comfortable profit, most of which did not turn up on the accounts but went straight into Delia's pocket as living expenses. She was once a talented stylist, but her ideas had largely become outdated. Occasionally she went on a course, but little changed. To Mak's way of thinking, that was what was wrong with her. Nothing changed. Dearest in 1980 was the same Dearest now. She said the same things and thought the same thoughts. Janis and Joe had been well cared for, and both parents loved them they were small.

Mak's leaving, once the relationship began to fall apart, ended the noise and the fighting. He was touring a lot, and his life was exciting. Delia was not much to look forward to when he got home. By then, he had seen Pattie and knew she was different. He did not consider that Delia might be bored by her life in the hairdressers and the demands of two children. He escaped, but he did not consider that she might want to run away too.

That was the trouble with Mak. He saw the world from one perspective, his own. He was a good musician, with all the natural instincts and stage presence of a talented performer.

Early on, when the lead singer drank himself into a final coma, Mak took the spotlight. The name remained the same as a tribute to their dead colleague, who at least lived and died like a rock and roll legend. Mak was attractive, and he knew it. He was glib and witty, and he thought that should be enough to make him a star. But, sometimes an audience sees beyond all the banter and the patter. If you looked closely at Mak, he was cold and self-serving, and it showed at the edges. His public did not quite warm to him. They liked him; some fans adored him because he was good looking and sexy, but deep down he was not a man you wanted to live with. The coldness under the surface would eventually freeze any warmth and kill any passion.

Delia was glad when he left. She ruled her home, and as long as Mak paid all the bills and visited the kids regularly, she did not miss him. She had her daughter and her friends for company. Once Mak moved in with Pattie, life settled down to a routine. She was also part of his working life, and he saw her often. When the band's fortunes declined, and the recording company ended their contract, Pattie was the one who encouraged Mak to look for other jobs. She gave up her job with the record company, set up her own accounts business and devoted the rest of her time to Mak. He never knew why she did it and if Pattie was honest, she didn't either.

Now Mak saw a chance of getting ahead, of clearing his considerable debts and moving on. Pattie was tired of their life and wanted to move abroad. He had no idea if she had any money saved. She paid the rent and most of the bills, but if she made any money from her business, he was afraid to ask. Pattie and money were dark chasms he dare not cross.

He had seen a way to solve his problem. Once his Aunt's house sold, he could sell Delia's house, and then the kid's house. He would be debt free and maybe have some to spare. He thought the deal he had offered Delia was more than fair. He could not see why she did not grab the chance to own her home and be free of a husband she discarded long ago.

Somehow, Delia did not grasp what was on offer. He did not understand that being married to him was important to her. He was determined not to give in to her whims. The offer to buy his half of the family home at lower than the market value was the solicitor's idea, and he thought it was something Delia would jump at. The divorce was simply tidying up the loose ends and setting all parties off on a new path. So, if Delia would not see reason, she would have to be pushed. He was so tired of it all.

He could hear Pattie already at work in her office, so he made coffee, took her a cup and leaning on the desk, he watched her type, trying not to let her see that he was staring down her shirt. Pattie wore his old checked shirts at home. They were warm and comfortable, worn with leggings for a day in her office. Her breasts nestled warmly inside the soft fabric. She was not big-breasted like Delia. She was neat and curvy. Mak loved her body; it did not provoke or confront; it invited and comforted.

'Toast?' he asked her.

Pattie looked up and smiled.

'Is that a new way of offering me a quickie?'

Mak grinned.

'Could be. Want to hop on the desk?'

'You are a wicked seducer, and I will not give into your evil desires unless I am fed. Toast first please.'

Mak kissed the top of her head.

'Cold, hard woman. Your servant obeys.'

While Mak was making the toast, Pattie suddenly thought that maybe the old Mak had returned. Once the houses sold and the debts were gone, they could leave and never come back. No more Delia and bingo club. They could leave it all. The dream she had when she first fell in love with Mak would finally be real.

Mak delivered the toast, and after another kiss, he left Pattie to her work while he went to the room known as the Music Room. This was where Mak kept his guitars and all the associated equipment. He had a desk and an old computer where he stored all his music files. His laptop was new, and he compiled the material for his sets and the part of his music library he used for the bingo club. He kept it away from Pattie, as it was occasionally used for things he did not want her to see. A bit of porn made up for his failing performance in bed. Not that it helped much. Now the groupies were getting less attractive. Trips to RedTube were all part of being a rock musician, according to Mak's way of thinking. It was all quite legal, but somehow, he did not want Pattie to find out. Her disappointment would be unbearable.

He set up his guitars and spent an hour or so practising as he noted down songs for the Saturday night set. Once he had put together a reasonable list, he emailed it to the rest of the band. Nothing complicated, as it was unlikely that Marilyn would let Peter play this weekend, so they were one short. He wished Joe were interested in music. It would be so good to have his son in the band. He was not even sure that his son had ever learned to play the guitar. He played some more, his fingers still responding as they always had. He still had his touch, even if his amp was making a strange noise. Another expense. Switching to an acoustic guitar, he played some flamenco, which soothed him and yet fired up a passion in him. Flamenco had passion and anger. Mak thought about his ex-wife and put his guitar down. He had all the anger he needed right now. Why could this not be easy? What was wrong with Dearest? He just wanted an end to all the needs and the arguments.

He flicked on RedTube and watched some very compli-cated sex in a basement between 'lusty teens and fit German backpackers'. It all seemed very unlikely, and the lack of passion rather put him off. He didn't remember sex being that dull, but then he often saw it through a haze of alcohol and drugs in the old days. He was sure it was fun, but mostly he could not remember their faces. Apart from Pattie, he could only remember Dearest, and he wanted to forget her for good.

———

TUESDAY 14 FEBRUARY

The following Tuesday morning dawned freezing cold. Mak was up early and warming himself with coffee before he headed over to the kid's house to meet the estate agent. Pattie was still asleep, so he took her a coffee and sat on the bed beside her to see if she woke up. She did not stir, so he left the cooling coffee, so she knew he had made it for her. Before he left, he stroked her shiny hair that spread over the pillow. It was Valentine's Day. He would buy her some roses.

'Doing this for you, darlin',' he whispered as he closed the door gently.

He collected the red toaster he had retrieved from Aunt Maud's house. It was still in the box. Pattie had complained it was in the way and had put it in the cupboard. He resealed the top of the box. He would give that to Janis to deliver to Dearest. No sense in putting himself in range of her anger. He stood for a moment in thought as if he was trying to decide something and then put on his outdoor coat. His Jag was on its last legs. The bodywork needed a lot of repairs, and the electrics had got damp during a big spell of rain when the car sat in water for a couple of days. He did love that car. It reminded him of the days when there was so much to look forward to. Other band members bought big sports cars, long since traded in for vans and family cars. Mak's Jag had survived as the last remnant of his brilliant career. When things were sorted out, he would have a new car.

He drove slowly through the icy streets and parked outside the kid's house. He had a set of keys, but as he wanted both of them up and ready when the estate agent arrived, he rattled the door loudly as he entered. Inside, Janis had attempted to tidy up, and he had only to remove the remains of Joe's late-night pizza from the coffee table and wash up some cups. As he was making coffee, Janis wandered down stairs.

'Morning Dad. You are up early. What happened to the rock and roll lifestyle?'

'It had kids, and they needed feeding.'

'Well, you long since stopped doing that, didn't you?' she sneered.

'I thought your business was going fine?'

'It's okay, I suppose. Too many Princesses. They want glitter and sequins and each nail a different pattern these days. It takes hours to do, and they expect it for the same price as regular nails. And it looks stupid unless they are going to a party.'

'How do they do the housework and wash up these days?' asked Mak, thinking of Pattie's neat cream nails slowly trailing across his chest.

'They don't, Dad. Not unless they have to.'

Mak was quiet, thinking of Pattie's fingers. He was thinking that he might have fewer problems getting an erection once the money worries had gone. That would make Pattie happy.

'What's that Dad?' Janis indicated the new toaster on the workbench.

'Aunt Maud's toaster from Argos - never even opened. Thought your mum might want it.'

'Right. Well, that might perk her up then.' Janis looked at

the box as if it might explode. 'I will drop it round. She needs something to cheer her up.'

'Yea right. Being rid of me should make her happy then.'

The doorbell rang before the sniping got worse and Mak went to open it. On the doorstep was the estate agent, a Ms Nikki Jones. She was smartly dressed in a blue suit, high-heeled shoes and no stockings. She looked glamorous but frozen. Mak ushered her into the kitchen and offered coffee. She accepted but looked critically at the state of the kitchen. Janis emerged from upstairs dressed in tracksuit and trainers. Mak introduced her, and they settled at the kitchen table to discuss the sale.

Ms Jones was shown the house once Joe was woken up and chased out of his room. He wandered downstairs in a dressing gown and his bright green gloves. He went into the kitchen and shook the toaster in its box before he lost interest and made himself some coffee. Ms Jones regarded him with disgust and quickly took photographs. She seemed confident that a buy-to-let purchaser would come along quickly if the price was right.

'I will just do the externals,' she said as was leaving, 'and then send the sales contract to you. Get this one on the market, and I think we can get a quick sale. When is the family leaving?'

'When we feel like it,' Janis snapped, eyeing the woman's immaculate blue nails.

The estate agent retreated to her car. It was best not to know too much about the family situation.

'What will you do, Janis?' asked Mak.

'When you make us homeless, you mean? I'm moving in with Mum. Joe is going to Manchester, he says.'

'Well let me know what it costs, luv, and I'll pay to get your stuff moved and anything you need.'

'Thanks, Dad.'

Mak felt guilty, but he would make sure both kids had some money from the sales. Not a lot, but enough to help them get by. It was time Joe got a job, and Janis worked harder on her own business or went back to work in a salon in town. The two were silent for a while. It was not an easy silence. Janis looked at her Dad and wished he had been an ordinary man, a plumber or an electrician, anything but a failed rock star. People at school had thought it was wonderful to have someone like Mak as a father. 'Your Dad is so good-looking. My mum fancies him like mad. Says he was really sexy when he was young.'

Janis was embarrassed. His music did not interest her, and she was ashamed that he had become just a second-rate performer in the local pubs and clubs. She loved him when she was little; loved the presents he brought her. When Pattie arrived on the scene, all that ended, and her Dad was gone and had stopped loving her.

———

SUNDAY 19 FEBRUARY

I t had been quiet for a few days. Delia's daily calls to Mak had slowed somewhat, and Pattie was hoping she had come to see reason. Life would be better without Delia always being part of their relationship. Pattie could not remember a time when Mak's ex-wife had not been part of their lives. When Pattie moved in with Mak, there had been a lot of anger, but this calmed down, and Pattie was pretty sure that Delia preferred an absent husband to a present, and often difficult, one. The two women came to a silent truce. Pattie did the accounts and relations were cold and formal and remained so until the question of the divorce came up. Pattie would be happy when it was all settled, and she and Mak could truly have a life of their own.

She was up early that morning and was hoping to catch up on some work before Mak got up. She put the washing in and settled down in the kitchen with a cup of coffee and her iPad. She read the news and then, realising the device was running very slowly, she fetched Mak's laptop from its case in the hall and did the online shopping for the next week. She didn't often use Mak's machine, but her room with the big desktop computer was cold. She preferred to stay warm in the kitchen. She clicked the order and made a note of the reference number and delivery day.

She was about to access another news site when she noticed the apps of a couple of websites she had read about in the news recently. She clicked on one and a splash page of writhing, naked bodies appeared on the screen. Pattie stared in disgust. She had seen porn sites before, but this was on Mak's laptop. She watched the images of men and women, intimate parts in dreadful shades of distorted flesh tones. The girls looked very young. The captions announced, 'Sexy teens have fun in foursome', and 'Mother and daughter join forces and get a big cock each.' She felt sick and saddened. This was a world without love or respect. Did it give Mak pleasure? Did it arouse him like she couldn't? Pattie closed the site and switched off the laptop. She went into the bathroom, and after staring at herself in the mirror for a few minutes, she leant over the toilet and was sick.

Later, she returned to the kitchen to find Mak making himself some coffee.

'Want some?'

'No thanks, Mak.'

She decided that she did not want to discuss the porn sites. There was no point. Mak would deny it and what could she say? He was doing nothing wrong. Nothing that men everywhere didn't do every day. Why should Mak be any different?

'You alright darlin'? Mak looked concerned.

'Sure, you will get your lunch, never fear.'

'Not what I meant, and you know it,' Mak snapped back.

Pattie decided to change the subject.

'I borrowed your laptop to do the shopping. My iPad is running slow again.'

'No problem, darlin'. Don't delete my music, will you?'

Pattie looked annoyed.

'Okay, okay, I know you wouldn't do that. You know more about computers than I do. Come here and give me a cuddle.'

He smiled his magical lopsided smile and held out his arms for her. After a moment, Pattie went towards him and sunk her head on his chest. She was so tired of everything. This was her life, all of it. She had chosen it when she fell in love with Mak. Our decisions come back to haunt us, right or wrong.

They spent a quiet day together watching TV, drinking a glass of wine or two, warm inside away from the cold winter winds. Pattie made an early dinner and loaded the dishwasher, while Mak played some music on his laptop that he was planning to use for the next set. Pattie had a good ear, and he trusted her opinion. If a song did not work, she would spot it and say so. Her musical taste was always a good barometer.

About six o'clock, the doorbell rang. They looked at each other. No one was expected, and they did not want visitors right now. Mak went to the door. Pattie could hear Delia's raised voice as soon as the door opened.

'A fucking toaster? Are you being funny, Mak? Is this a consolation prize? She gets my husband. I get a toaster? Is that supposed to be funny?'

'Come in and sit down, Dearest. I gave you the toaster because I thought you might like it. No other reason. Let's talk this through quietly now.'

Mak was trying to steer her away from the kitchen, but realising Pattie was in there, she pushed past him.

The two women glared at each other. Pattie felt drained and exhausted. One last fight and we might be rid of Delia. She took a deep breath.

'You can have a glass of wine, or I can make you a cup of coffee, Delia. But you are not shouting and yelling in our home.

Delia waited and considered the offer.

'And this is *our* home. Mine and Mak's. We make the rules here, not you. So, sit down and listen to me for once.'

Delia still made no move.

'Okay, stand then. This is how it is. Mak is not your husband anymore. He has not been your husband for ten years. So, it is time to end this charade once and for all. He has made you a fair offer on the house, and you can take it or leave it. You cannot stop the divorce. It will happen, with or without you. But what we do want is you, out of our lives. Mak is selling up, and we are moving on, and we are not taking you with us. Mak has carried you this far, and it is time to end it. Now.'

Delia was shaking with anger and trying to find some words to throw back at Pattie to match the ones she had just heard. They hurt, and Pattie had meant them to. Pattie stood leaning against the workbench, her face flushed but determined. Mak looked at the two women, and like most men faced with this situation, he was helpless. All he could do was watch.

Delia wanted with all her heart for Mak to come to her, tell her he was wrong, and didn't want Pattie rather than her. She could also see that it would never happen. Mak had chosen Pattie, and it was time for her to let go. But she couldn't. She pushed past Mak and marched to the door, slamming it behind her.

Pattie sat down and put her head in her hands.

'I just want you to this to end, Mak, and I don't care how you do it.'

———

WEDNESDAY 22 FEBRUARY

Mak knew what his audience liked, but it was not a case of churning out the same old stuff. He also wanted to play the music he enjoyed. The same music every week could make for a dull time. The bingo club was not a top venue, but he always hoped for better things. He recorded the best sets, and when he had the enthusiasm, he sent copies off to radio stations in the hope of a job.

The club was full every week, and it was not just for the bingo and the food. Mak told them about the music and the audience enjoyed being treated as knowledgeable adults; it did not happen too often in a world where the older you become, the more frequently you were patronised by some receptionist or nurse or social worker. Pattie had long since given up telling people that she was not their 'luv'.

Back in the Fifties, the American singer Buddy Holly was a huge favourite in England. He had been popular when alive and now he was dead, his memory still burned brightly. Mak had put together what he like to call 'the air crash set', which celebrated the music of all those who had died in plane crashes going to and from gigs in the USA. Pattie thought it was a bit gruesome, but admired Mak wanting to give his audience something better than the average.

They arrived early at the club as Pattie had created some slides, with pictures of each artist, to put on the screen behind the stage. Mak seemed better now. His energy had increased, and although Aunt Maud's house had not sold, plenty of people were viewing it, so it was only a matter of time before he got a sale.

Mak had been clear in his instructions to sell the house to someone who would not delay the sale. It was not the sort of house that attracted the buy-to-let market, those who just wanted to tart it up and exploit renters. The kid's place would attract that type of unscrupulous buyer and would sell fast. Aunt Maud's house was a family home, modern with a nice garden. Mak got a builder to fill in the fishpond and pave over it. The ornamental pond where his Aunt had drowned was not the sort of feature to attract the buyers. Pattie still watched him anxiously and helped him avoid the frequent calls from Delia, who was still insisting that Mak could not divorce her. She would listen eventually, but for now, she was making as much fuss as she could. It was a matter of pride for her to remain married to Mak, and she simply did not understand that the divorce was inevitable. The kids had phoned a few times to argue the case for staying in the house, but Mak said no, he had made up his mind. Pattie thought it was good to see him being positive for once.

The club filled up, and everyone settled down to the bingo while Mak and Pattie sat at the bar. The event was advertised locally, and a few Buddy Holly fans had come along, complete with the horn-rimmed glasses. Once the bingo was over, Pattie put on the slides and Mak started with 'American Pie' to huge applause and out of tune singing. This lot knew every word.

Good afternoon everybody and welcome to Wednesday with Mak and welcome to everyone out there on Long Time Radio available twenty-four seven on longtimeradio.com. So, Happy Wednesday, I got a load of music lined up for this very special set, which I call 'the Day the Music Died'.

First up was a song that you all know, 'American Pie' by Don Maclean. I think, by the way you were all singing along, that it is one of your all-time favourites.

So, a bit of music history for you. Don Maclean was aged 13, and he was folding newspapers for his paper round on the morning of February 4 when he first learned that his idol Buddy Holly had died in a plane crash the day before on February 3, 1959.

Buddy Holly was the headline act on the tour and his plane crashed at Clear Lake, Iowa, killing all aboard, including the young Latin heartthrob Ritchie Valens; the Big Bopper, who was a singer and DJ by the name of JP Richardson; and the pilot, Roger Peterson.

I think some of you remember that day too. Not you ladies, of course. You are all much too young.

So today I have put together some of the best tunes from artists who have died in plane crashes. Yes, that's right, plane crashes and there seem to be quite a lot of them.

So, first up are two of your favourite tunes by Buddy Holly and the Crickets, 'That'll Be the Day' and 'Peggy Sue'.

With the first notes the audience were up dancing, and the years seems to fall away from middle-aged women in too-tight jeggings jiving expertly with balding men, who got quickly out of puff. These were the happy songs of their school days, and you could see by their faces that many would go back tomorrow if only they could. Life, in most cases, had been a disappointment and knowing what they knew now, they would like to go back for a second crack at it.

Delia did not want a second crack at it. She had not finished with the first. She never went to Mak's sets. She has a business to run, as she frequently told Paulina as they sat in the salon with the sole customer, drinking tea. It was 3 pm, and she would go home soon and leave Paulina to clean the sinks and lock up. Her assistant was then obliged to drop the keys in as she walked past Delia's house on her way home. Delia did not trust Paulina with the keys, and her apprentice did not care that much. The work was easy, and she had no responsibility. Her plans were to work until she married and then do nothing once she had a baby. Life for Paulina had no distant horizons. She was left to wash up, while Delia put on her coat with the extravagant fur collar and made her way home. The house was warm, and she thought she would have an early bath, put on her fleecy dressing gown and have cheese on toast in front of the TV.

The dancers staggered back to their chairs and reached for their drinks. Most were sure that they were as fit as when they were twenty, but clearly, they were not. Time had marched on unkindly.

I can see that you all enjoyed that. So, let's move right on to something a bit slower. Ritchie Valens was the first of the Spanish-speaking rock and roll movement. During his short career, he had several hits, most notably 'La Bamba'. You all remember that one, don't you? Ritchie Valens was just eighteen years old when he died alongside Buddy and the Big Bopper on that day in 1959. This is his hit song, 'Donna'.

Kit Colley had arrived quietly and got himself a drink. He was off duty, had seen the poster in the kebab shop, and was curious to hear about Mak's interesting set. He was a fan of Buddy Holly, had all the records, on forty-fives too, although it was not something he admitted to. Then there was Pattie, and he did have an idea that he would like to check on how she and Mak were going since Aunt Maud's sudden death. He watched the sweaty dancers cling to each other as they moved around the dance floor to the smooth tones of Ritchie Valens. Great voice; gone too soon.

The next song is one that makes you get up and jive. This man was a pioneer of rockabilly. J.P. Richardson was a singer and DJ, known as the Big Bopper, and this is his hit song, which he also co-wrote 'Chantilly Lace'.

The serious dancers were back on the floor, and the Buddy Holly fans took time off at the bar. KC looked around for Pattie and found her at a side table dressed in her usual black. He approached in slow stages, not wanting Mak to see him. He wondered exactly why he was doing this and why the older woman was so attractive to him. Something was in the air and had been since the death of Aunt Maud. Once he got an itch, KC obeyed its call until he tired of it and moved on.

There you go. That got you moving, didn't it? Maybe you think that we can't all die like Buddy Holly. Well, actually we can. He was not the only American singer to die tragically in a plane crash. This next song is by the country singer, Patsy Cline. Cline's flight crashed in heavy weather on the evening of March 5, 1963, in a forest outside Camden, Tennessee. Her wristwatch, recovered from the crash, had stopped at six twenty. Just a bit of trivia for you there. You all know this famous country blues song, 'Walkin' After Midnight'.

Pattie saw KC at the bar and was determined not to acknowledge his presence. As he moved toward her table, she had trouble suppressing her lifting spirits. She had an uncomfortable feeling that he was not here just for the music. She nodded to him as he indicated the empty chair opposite to hers and sat down. They did not speak, but both looked towards Mak. KC was studying the grainy black-and-white photo behind the stage of Patsy Cline, and Pattie was watching Mak to see if he had noticed KC's arrival.

So let's move on. Ricky Nelson dreaded flying but refused to travel by bus, cos he was a big star. He decided he needed a private jet, like you do, and leased a luxurious fourteen-seat, Douglas DC-3. Only the plane had a bit of a history of mechanical problems. In December 1985, Nelson and the band left for a three-stop tour of the Southern United States. The plane crash-landed in Texas on New Year's Eve, hitting trees as it came down to earth. Seven of the nine occupants died, including Ricky Nelson. This is his famous song 'Hello Mary Lou'.

Delia had a nice hot bath with lots of bubbles. She was trying not to think about Mak today, but her anger bubbled away just under the surface. She did not want to be divorced; she had made up her mind about that. She reasoned that Mak would give way eventually if she kept on at him. He always did. At least, he always had in the past. The last attempt had not gone so well. She tried calling Janis to make her talk to her father again, but Janis was just sulking, and Joe was talking about moving to a squat in Manchester. She lay in the warmth as the bath water drained away and then reached for her fluffy towel and wrapped herself in the soft folds.

The set was going well, and the club owner was praising Mak to his customers at the bar. They were getting hot and buying more beer, which was how he liked it.

So now we come to one of my favourites. He is a great guitarist, and I wish I could play half as well as him. He is still remembered and played by all who love the blues. Stevie Ray Vaughan was aged only 35 when he died. On August 27, 1990, Vaughan performed two shows with Eric Clapton in East Troy, Wisconsin. Some of the musicians boarded helicopters, which were waiting on a nearby golf course. Despite the conditions, the pilots flew over a 1000-foot ski hill into which the helicopter carrying Vaughan and some of Clapton's entourage crashed with no survivors. This is one of my favourite songs. You have all heard me play this before. This is the very talented and very dead Stevie Ray Vaughan with one of his most popular songs, 'Pride and Joy.

'So how are you, Pattie?' KC asked.

'I am well, thank you.'

Pattie did not want to encourage him, and yet she wanted to talk to him. Missing from her life was someone who saw the world outside the bingo club and Saturday nights in the pub.

'I see probate went smoothly and Mak has put his Aunt's house on the market. Should fetch a few bob, nice house like that.'

'I don't really know, only went inside a couple of times. Maud kept it nice. They think about four forty thousand or thereabouts.'

'Wow, that will make a nice windfall for Mak, I expect.'

Pattie was not sure why he said that.

'I am sure he did not want his Aunt to die in such an awful way just to provide him with a windfall.'

She looked annoyed.

KC looked back towards the screen at the boyish face of Stevie Ray Vaughan. He enjoyed this music. The man's talent smacked you right in the face every time you heard him play, which was not often on the mainstream radio stations. Why was he needling Pattie about Mak's Aunt's death? He was not sure, but somehow an accidental drowning in an ornamental fishpond after a few too many drinks did not seem right to him. Those were the pathologist's findings, so he should just let it go. He looked back at Pattie. She looked tired, sad, and not inclined to talk to him.

Delia put on her new snuggly animal-print dressing gown; Marks and Sparks' best. It had been a Christmas present from Janis. She thought that her daughter might have inherited her own good taste. The house was warm and cosy, and she went downstairs to check the TV guide and plan her night's viewing. Next week, she would see her solicitor again and try to make him understand that she wanted to contest the divorce. Surely, she could do that.

She went through to the kitchen and realised she had no cheese in the fridge. So, no cheese on toast then. She scowled into the cupboard, wondering what else she might have. Finding a jar of Nutella, she placed it on the worktop and took four slices of bread from the bread bin. On the table was the toaster that Mak had brought from his Aunt Maud's. He had bought it for his Aunt shortly before her death, and she had never used it, poor old lady. The box lid was only sealed with sellotape, so Delia peeled it back, lifted the toaster out of the packaging and removed the cable ties and bits of cardboard holding it firm. She cut the box up and put the folded it ready for the recycling.

'Brilliant guitar playing. I gather he is one of Mak's heroes. One of mine too, actually.'

Pattie looked up. She thought he was trying to soften his previous comments.

'Mine too,' she agreed. 'I was in the music business when I

met Mak, in accounts, but I got to hear a lot of concerts. Never heard Stevie Ray play live, sadly, but his music has been a bit of a soundtrack to life with Mak.'

'That and Clapton, I expect.'

Pattie smiled at him for the first time since he had sat down.

'Yes and Clapton.'

They sat in silence. There was no need to speak. They could both feel it. It was more than attraction; it was temptation. One significant word or smile and there would be no going back. The music was luring them both. Pattie kept her eyes fixed on Mak. This was her man for good or worse, and she had come too far now to change things now. Finally, KC reluctantly whispered his goodbye and went to drink at the bar. She didn't see him leave the club, but she knew he was gone and part of her regretted it.

Now we get to a singer that you all know, Otis Redding. In 1967, Redding and his band were travelling to performances in Redding's plane. The weather was poor, heavy rain and fog, and despite the warnings, the plane took off. Why none of them listen to the weather forecasts, I do not know. Four miles from their destination in Madison, the pilot radioed for permission to land. Shortly after, the plane crashed into Lake Monona. Redding was just twenty-six years old. This is the song we all remember him for 'The Dock of the Bay'.

The audience was getting romantic now. They enjoyed these songs. A few might be thinking hopefully of getting her husband home and making him something nice for his supper and having an early night. Their husbands were considering a nap in front of the box.

. . .

Well, there were a lot of intimate moments going on during that song and here's another to get you hugging your partner tight. On Friday, July 31, 1964, country singer Jim Reeves and his business partner left Batesville, Arkansas, en route to Nashville in a single-engine aircraft, with Reeves at the controls. They were flying over Tennessee when they ran into a violent thunderstorm and crashed. The wreckage was found some forty hours later. You might not remember him too well, but you will remember this song. This is the wonderful voice of the late, great Jim Reeves singing 'I Love You Because'.

The new toaster was bright red. Delia placed it in the spot where her old toaster had been. She wound the cord around the base and positioned it so it could be plugged in. She switched it on, put the bread in and dropped the lever down. The elements warmed up and she adjusted the knobs. The cable was not sitting on the base properly. The toast popped up, and she put it on the plate and then turned the toaster on to its side to push the cables back into the base. Her hand reached round to the point where the cable exited from the black plastic base. She only saw the raw wires the moment her fingers touched them. Her body went rigid as the current flowed through her. There were no last thoughts.

Paulina washed down the sinks and swept the floor. It was five thirty, and she was thinking of going home to her mum's and having a nice dinner and an evening of television. Life without effort worked well for her. She knew everything she needed to get by with the minimum of effort. She wrapped herself in her padded coat, wrapping a scarf around the hood and pulling on two pairs of wool gloves.

After she had checked all the sockets were switched off, Delia was very particular about that. She turned off the main light switch and locked the door. It would take her about ten minutes to reach Delia's house. She would ring the bell and hand over the keys. Very occasionally her employer invited her in, but usually, she just wanted to get home. She saw enough of Dearest at work.

The roads were slippery with sleet and Paulina snuggled into her hood and hurried along, careful that she did not slip on the uneven pavements. When she reached Delia's house, it was clear, even to Paulina, that something was not right. The lights were on upstairs and down, including the porch light, but the curtains were not drawn as they normally were in the room facing the street. Delia was fussy about things like that. 'Can't have people seeing all you got', she would giggle suggestively, presuming anyone wanted to look.

Paulina rang the bell and then, when she got no answer, she peered into the high front window. She could faintly see the kitchen lights beyond, but no sign of Delia. She tried both phone numbers and could hear them ringing faintly inside. She was just about to put the shop keys through the letter box when it occurred to her that her employer might have slipped in the bath. She knew Delia was planning a bath because she was shown the newly purchased jasmine bubble bath.

Paulina stood for a moment wondering what to do and then reached into her pocket for her mobile and called Janis. After a few rings, Janis answered and listened impatiently while Pauline went into detail, including the brand of bubble bath. Janis swore and said she would come over straight away. Paulina protested that she was cold and would leave the shop keys and go home.

'No, Paulina, you will stay right there. What if Mum suddenly answers the door, and I have traipsed all that way for nothing? You stay there and call me if she shows up.'

So, Paulina tucked herself into the porch while she called her mother to say she might be late. After about fifteen minutes, Janis arrived with the keys to the house. She unlocked, and the two women went inside to get out of the cold. The house was very quiet. Janis called out a couple of times, but there was no reply.

'Spooky,' said Pauline, in a high voice.

'Stupid cow, get a grip,' said Janis.

Neither moved. Then Janis went into the room and towards the front window, and after looking outside briefly, she closed the curtains. When she turned, she was looking directly into the kitchen, and there was no doubt about what she saw.

Delia was lying on the floor against the cupboards. Her body was rigid. Janis considered her next move. She was no coward and some of the things that ran through her head at that moment were what she might wear for the funeral and whether she would get her mum's share of the house. To give Janis the benefit of the doubt, it could be assumed to be shock and the finer feelings of love and loss would soon overcome her sudden callous reaction. She returned to the hall and Paulina.

'I think Mum has had an accident and we better call an ambulance. Just wait there Paulina, while I make the calls.'

Paulina didn't argue. She could tell by the look on Janis's face that something was very wrong. Her tea would be cold. Once the call was made, the two sat on the stairs facing the front door and did not speak until the sirens could be heard. Janis opened the door and let the para- medics in. Then she returned to sit on the stairs beside Paulina. The two women sat close, saying nothing and anxiously waiting for someone to tell them what to do next. A woman in a luminous yellow jacket came and asked their names and the name of the women in the kitchen. Then she got on her radio and called for the police to attend and gave the address.

'Your Mum?' she asked Janis.

Janis nodded.

'I think you should prepare yourself for a shock, ducks. Mum has had a bad accident. Nothing we can do to help her.

100

Police are on their way, so you just sit here and stay calm till they arrive.'

Paulina put her arm around Janis's shoulder, and the two tried not to shiver. As the shock set in, neither could find the right words. Once the police arrived, Janis and Paulina were taken upstairs to sit in the bedroom, while a policewoman brought them two mugs of tea and stood by the door. It was not clear if they were being guarded or if she was keeping them company. Finally, it all got too much for Paulina, and she started to sob that she wanted her tea.

After an hour, KC arrived, alerted by the uniform officers that another death had occurred in Mak Mason's family. He looked into the upstairs room and acknowledged the two women. Then he went downstairs and looked at the body.

'Everyone out of the kitchen,' he ordered. 'I want a forensic team in here ASAP. And whoever made tea needs to make sure we have their fingerprints and DNA. Get a cordon set up outside. No media and no statements.'

'This a crime scene, KC?'

'Don't know, but the truth is rarely pure and never simple.'

'That one of your quotes, KC,' asked the sergeant.

'You know me well,' said KC. 'The immoral Oscar himself.'

'Of course, I was gonna say that,' said the sergeant, heading for the door to get things moving.

KC sat with Janis for a while before she was ready to speak. Paulina was taken home with strict instructions that she should discuss the events with no one and if asked, was to say Mrs Mason had an accident. He was pretty sure that Paulina could add nothing further to Janis's evidence.

'So tell me in your own words, Janis, what you did when

Paulina called you to say she was getting no answer at your Mum's house.'

'I put my coat and boots on and came straight over here. It's only about ten minutes; not far, really. Joe was upstairs, so I just shouted that I was going round to Mums. He didn't answer, but then he mostly doesn't.'

KC could see the shock setting in. Any useful questions must be asked while she could still remember.

'So tell me exactly what you did. Step by step.'

'I unlocked the door and called out. Mum didn't answer. It didn't feel right, you know.'

She slowed down and sat for a moment, not speaking.

'So, what did you do next?'

'I told Paulina to stay in the hall, and I went into the front room. I went straight to the window, looked out and drew the curtains. It keeps the heat in, you know. Then I turned, and you can see into the kitchen. She had the two rooms knocked into one with just glass doors. Looks so much nicer. I looked into the kitchen, and she was just lying by the bench. I just knew, you know. I knew.'

'You knew she was dead, Janis? Did you go in?'

'I knew, didn't need to look, so I went back to the hall and called for an ambulance.'

Janis was crying now.

'You didn't go into the kitchen, see if she was alive, maybe?'

'No, I knew you see, I knew.'

'How did you know, Janis? What made you so certain?'

Janis looked at him angrily, as if he was stupid

'She looked like a body at Pompeii. Like you see on TV. She was stiff, frozen. I knew, alright, I knew.'

Death for Janis was something she had seen on TV. KC wished that was all the death he had seen. Mangled bodies in needless car crashes made him feel sick. A dead child gutted you for days.

'Alright, Janis. I am going to get an officer to take you

home and tell your brother. They will stay with you until you are okay. Alright?'

Janis nodded.

'Tomorrow I will get you, and we can look around the house and see if you can see anything out of the ordinary. I will call your Dad. No need for you to worry tonight.'

She nodded again but was no longer listening to him.

———

THURSDAY 23 FEBRUARY

Next morning KC was at the house early. The forensic team had worked until late, and the body was removed. He sent the constable to fetch coffees and stood alone in the kitchen, looking around. The room had an odd quality, like someone had recently left and would return any minute. The suspect toaster was still on the workbench. It was new and bright red, as were some of the other appliances. KC had never seen a red refrigerator before, but obviously, the colour appealed to Delia.

By the waste bin was a carefully folded box that had contained the new toaster. Forensics would collect the items that morning, but first he wanted to walk Janis through the kitchen. She would know it best. He settled down on the sofa and arranged for her to be collected and driven to the house. Then he phoned Mak Mason. He was the ex-husband after all, so KC had waited before making the call. Maybe Janis had called already.

Pattie answered the phone, and KC asked if Janis had called her father.

'No, why. What's happened?'

'I can tell you, or I can tell Mak if you prefer. It concerns his wife.'

'Ex-wife,' corrected Pattie. Taking a deep breath, she went on, 'You better tell me.'

'I am sorry to tell you that Mrs Mason died last night in an accident at her home.'

Pattie was silent.

'You still there, Pattie?'

'Sure, you want me to tell, Mak?'

'Please, if you would, and I will be around to see him later this morning, if that is okay. By the way, were you both at home last night after the bingo?'

'Yes. Yes, we were. Mak would have better things to do than murder Delia, even if she was a pain in the ass.'

'I am sure he has, Pattie. It was an accident, we think. I'll let you tell him then. I'll text before I come over.'

'Sure, we will be here.'

KC ended the call. Any relationship he might have imagined having with Pattie was now merely a fantasy. Mak would need her now, more than ever, and Pattie would respond by giving him all her love and support. What a waste of a lovely woman. He was not sure what he had been hoping for. Pattie was older than him, intelligent, capable but trapped like a caged bird. He just wanted to see her fly free. And now that would not happen.

There was a sound at the door, and the sergeant arrived with Janis and her brother. Both looked confused and shaken; Joe, more so than his sister. He went to the hall to meet them and let them into the front room. The glass doors into the kitchen were closed. Janis looked towards them anxiously.

'How you are guys doing today? Alright? Let me know if there is anything we can do. You got a family liaison officer coming around later to help you through the early days. This morning, I want you to help me establish a few facts. Mostly you, Janis, as you would know the house pretty well, I think.'

He stood and led her to the glass doors. Janis flinched.

'Okay, all I want is for you to look around the kitchen and tell me if anything is different from usual.'

'My Mum was dead on the fucking floor,' snapped Janis, 'that is a bit unusual, don't you think?'

'I know you are upset, and that is natural. Let's just look, shall we, and then you can go home.'

He opened the doors and led her in. Janis looked around the kitchen but would not go in.

'Well, the toaster is new. I bought that over for her on the weekend. There's the box over there with the recycling. The old toaster was getting on, so she had the new one that Dad had got from Argos for Aunt Maud. He said it might cheer her up.'

'And everything else is just as normal? Was the box sealed when your Dad gave it to you?'

'Sure.'

She looked sadly around the kitchen as if for the last time.

'She was hiding that Nutella from me, wicked cow.'

Janis stood in the doorway and sobbed.

Once Janis and Joe had left, the forensic officer arrived to collect the toaster, and the discarded wrappings. He turned the toaster over and showed KC the melted cable that had caused the fatal accident.

'Strange for new equipment, don't you think?'

'It happens. Quality control fails or, more often, it is a returned item, and no one checks before it goes back on sale. Got a lot of finger prints last night and we will check the packing and establish who opened it and when. Should be able to tell if has been resealed. Best you let the local supplier know just in case they have a dodgy batch.'

'Righty-oh. Quick as you can. I got a date with the pathologist.'

KC hated dead bodies, and he had seen a few. The cheerful voice of the pathologist on the phone and made him wince.

'What you can tell me, and do I need to come down?'

'I don't think so, KC'. He chuckled, sensing KC's relief.

' Electrocution, clear and simple. Lady touched the bare wire with damp hands and lights out. Fast and efficient. Nothing to see here. Healthy female in her fifties, no injuries other than the burns where she touched the wires.'

'Does it strike you as odd,' suggested KC, 'that two women in the same family have both died in domestic accidents in the last three months?'

'Odd, but not beyond the realm of possibility, I should think. Why do you think the toaster was tampered with?'

'No reason to suppose it was, but I want to be sure. Mrs Mason didn't exactly have enemies, but she was a bit of a pain. Double check your double checks and hold on to that body for the moment. I want the coroner to look at this one.'

'Whatever you say, KC.'

KC sat for a while and considered the evidence so far. Then he called his team and set them to work, checking on the source of the toaster and doing the rounds to see if the neighbours had seen anything. Then he sent a text to Mak's phone to let them know he was on his way over.

Mak was still in bed when Pattie gently broke the news. He said nothing and went to the bathroom. When he returned, Pattie had made coffee, and both sat in the kitchen. Talking seemed pointless at this stage, and Pattie returned to her accounts until the text from KC flashed up to say he was on his way round. She returned to the kitchen, washed up and then prepared coffee. Mak was in his music room playing the guitar. She looked fondly at his figure wrapped around his treasured Gibson, one foot up on the amplifier, which rocked slightly as he played. Pattie put her arms around his shoulders and kissed his neck. She was finding it hard to speak.

'KC is on his way, luv. I'm making coffee. You come through when you are ready.'

'Thanks. This amp is popping. I'll drop it by the repair shop when we go into town next.'

'Sure, darlin'. I'll remind you.'

She could only talk of mundane, ordinary things. Delia's name was not mentioned. Neither were ready for that yet.

KC arrived, and Pattie showed him into the kitchen, knocking on the door for Mak as they walked past the room. She made three coffees and put out a plate of biscuits. Death makes you hungry, but you forget to eat. She was pretty sure that KC had missed breakfast. Neither she nor Mak felt like eating that morning. KC drank his coffee and got out his notebook.

'I am sorry to be the bearer of such bad news. Your ex-wife, Delia Mason, died last night around 6pm. Her body was discovered by your daughter Janis, who was called when your wife's apprentice could not get an answer to the doorbell.'

Mak looked up.

'Poor Janis. Is she alright? She didn't call me?'

'No, she was in shock. We took her home. It was best she didn't call. Nothing you could do last night.'

'Still, it was my kid's mother. You should have called me.'

'I felt it would serve no purpose. Your wife died by elec-trocution. We think the new toaster had exposed wires, which she touched with damp or wet hands. Death was instant.'

'And Janis found her. Poor kid.' Mak seemed very upset.

'Now,' continued KC, 'I need to track the route of that toaster. You bought it for your Aunt Maud, I believe, before she died?'

'If I remember correctly, Maud bought it online, and we collected it for her. I dropped it round the week she died.'

He looked at Pattie, who nodded in agreement.

'After Maud died, I brought a few things from the house; family pictures, some jewellery, TV and the new toaster. We didn't need a toaster and Delia likes red things. She's got a red fridge for some reason, so I gave it to Janis to drop round to her a week or so ago.'

'And the box. Was it sealed when you collected it from Argos?'

'Yes.'

'And when you collected from your Aunt's, had she opened it?'

'It was still in the packing. The tape on the top of the box was sliced open, so I resealed it with sellotape before I gave it to Janis.'

'And you didn't take the toaster out of the box to examine it?'

'No need. It was a new toaster. We didn't need it, so I took it over to Janis to give to her Mum.'

Mak was getting flustered.

'What is this exactly,' said Pattie. 'Is Mak accused of something here? That toaster arrived here in its box like it was new, and Mak took it over to Janis that way.'

'Not accusing Mak of anything here, Pattie. We need to know if the toaster was tampered with or there was a fault when it was collected from the store. That's all. Did you see if it was sealed?'

'It was not. But if Mak says Aunt Maud had cut open the lid to look at it, but did not take it out of the packaging, then that's what happened. If she cut along the tape, then stands to reason, he would seal it up before he took it to Janis, don't it?'

Pattie looked angrily at KC. Any desire she may have felt for him was rapidly disappearing. He was just an ambitious copper on the make.

'Don't worry, luv. He's got to ask us. I've lost two people in three months. This looks like a habit, don't it?'

'Exactly Mak, I have got to ask. If you can write down for me where you collected the toaster, we will get on to the store right away. Could be a faulty batch. I'll let you know. Also, I will need the tape you used to reseal the box and we will need to take your fingerprints and those of the Janis and Joe. I suggest you go see the kids today. Janis is in shock but is coping alright. I think Joe needs you. You might like to hold off on the sale of their place until they have buried their mum. The inquest will be fairly swift. I'll keep you informed.'

Pattie fetched the sellotape, the store details and then showed him out. She came back to the kitchen to find Mak staring out of the window at the grey sky.

———

TUESDAY 28 FEBRUARY

Rumours and innuendo, as they say, were fuelling the local gossip mill. The police released a brief statement, and the local paper had a page two banner headline, 'Popular local hairdresser dies in a freak accident'. Janis and Joe stayed home and drank, ate pizza and said little. Mak and Pattie carried on as usual. Pattie did not ask, and Make did not say, but something was wrong, and she could feel it. His sets at the bingo club were usually subdued, although he added a few songs in memory of Delia. One was the hugely popular new version of 'The Sound of Silence', the old Simon and Garfunkel song given a new interpretation by a metal band, Disturbed. Everyone sang along, but Pattie thought the choice of song was a bit inappropriate given Delia's volubility. Things were quiet without Delia.

The full report from the forensic team made for interesting, if inconclusive, reading. The company reported that all the toasters of that type had been immediately withdrawn from sale and tested by an independent laboratory. They had their reputation to consider and were sparing no expense to avoid a huge damage claim. None of the other toasters were found to be faulty and checks on other brands in the store ruled out a random sabotage or extortion attempt. The toaster likely had bare wires exposed at the point where the cable entered the base, or just where Delia had placed her damp fingers while winding up the cable. Forensic concluded that, either, although both unlikely, that the cable had not been properly screwed into the holding clamp beneath the base or the plastic casing had been damaged, exposing the live wires when Delia pulled the cable during unpacking. Or someone had tampered with the toaster.

The box was carefully examined and found to be just as Mak said. The tape sealing the top flaps had been slit open, but another strip had been placed over the top to secure the box. That tape was the same as the sample from Mak's place, and his fingerprints and those of Janis and Delia were on the shiny surface of the tape. Nothing could be found on the box or inside the packaging. On the outside of the toaster, they found only partial smudged prints and one or two clear finger-prints belonging to Delia.

KC had a couple of strong cups of coffee and circulated the report to his team for their input. The office was quiet for a while, but no one could come up with any new theories. It looked like Delia Mason had died by accidental electrocution. The question of who might benefit from Delia's death was unclear. There was no will, so it was likely that Janis and Joe would receive the proceeds from Delia's half of the house when the house was sold. Her shop was leased, so, for now, no decisions were being made, but the landlord, in a brief call, had suggested the Janis might take it over. KC had talked to the kids, and he thought it unlikely that either of them would harm their mother. Which left Mak. His wife was irritating him. He made no secret of that, but not enough to kill for, surely. The financial advantage was clear but not huge.

On the other hand, Mak would know how to open the

toaster and fix things, so the wires were exposed. He was also clever enough to realise that none of his prints or DNA must find its way inside the box. After another coffee, KC was still wondering. Supposing Mak had planned to kill his Aunt with the toaster. Then she conveniently got tipsy and drowned herself in her own fish pond. It would be simple to just pass the toaster on to Delia and rid himself of his annoying wife. But would he do that? He was a man under pressure, certainly. Maybe it was time to run a financial check to see just how bad things had become.

He crossed the office and arranged for one of the team to do a check on Mak Mason and all the rest of the family. It won't hurt to know. Then there was Pattie. Would the threat of losing her make a man kill? He sunk into his chair and put himself in Mak's shoes. If Pattie were his, he would fight to keep her. She was a treasure; he could see that. A woman like Pattie, clever, intelligent and patient, would make a man's life a joy. Would Mak kill to keep her? Would I kill to keep her, he wondered, and then dismissed the idea?

KC was in no hurry to find a permanent partner. His current girlfriend had extended her holiday, and he had an idea that a holiday romance was going on in the family villa. He did not ask because he did not care. She was fun, and the sex was active, but nothing special. Her return was irrelevant to him. He was intrigued by Pattie. He had hoped he might one day find an opportunity to sit and talk to her without Mak being around. Now it looked like he might get that opportunity for all the wrong reasons and none that would endear him to her.

He stared at her date of birth on file. She was fourteen years older than him. That was a huge gap, and so far, she had not exactly shown any interest other that seeming to enjoy his company. KC was fascinated by her, and he had no theory for his feelings. Did she know what he was thinking? Mak certainly did. His hostility was clear.

KC sighed loudly, and the rest of the team looked up. He stretched out his arms theatrically, and all eyes were on him.

'Financial checks.'

He pointed toward the woman allotted this task, then worked around the room.

'Recheck everyone's movements and neighbour's statements'.

'Check all CCTV for the local area on the night she died and see if the store has CCTV of the day Mak collected the toaster.'

'All got jobs? Let's put a fine-tooth comb through this one. I'm off the tackle Our Lady of Forensics in her lair. Report back this afternoon.'

KC put on his overcoat and a scarf and went out into the cold to walk around the block to the forensics lab.

England in February and March is a horrible place to live. The sky is dark most of the time; the weather is consistently cold and damp. A country of permanent gloom. When you looked out at the landscape, it seemed unlikely that anything would ever grow again. It was a picture of death, a black and white print yellowing at the edges, and it was hard to imagine that under the ground daffodils and crocus were ready to appear.

Brexit was biting and even those who naively thought it was a good idea wouls soon realise how much they were about to pay for their decision. Anyone with qualifications had already filled out their immigration papers. Europe was laughing at them, and those who could leave were thinking about pastures new. KC wondered what he should do. He was not good at languages so a transfer into Europe, while there was still time, was not likely. Policing was about to get harder now the bigots and racists were part of mainstream politics.

When the Leave camp realised how much harder things were about to get and that their holidays in Spain were more expensive and they had to pay for a visa, they would take their anger and frustration out onto the streets. Endless competitions on TV were fuelling a society full of self-interest and aggression. The young felt betrayed, and those who had no hope would resort to drugs, crime and the occasional riot. Not a good time to be a front-line police inspector. He shivered in the wind and hurried inside the forensic department. Once his pass was checked, he was sent downstairs to the warren of laboratories and offices to meet with the writer of the report.

Julia Winterton was very young. She had graduated three years earlier with a Master's in Forensic Science and spent a year in a big lab in Edinburgh. She was clever, focused and extremely inquisitive. She liked to get to the bottom of a problem and was not afraid to bounce around theories and scenarios to make sense of the confused bundle of evidence she had to sift through. She was very tall for a woman, over six feet. She towered above most of those around her and was known affectionately as the 'Supermodel'. She did look a little like Naomi Campbell, KC thought, and was at least four inches taller than he was. Like most men, he could not see himself with a much taller woman, but she had a grace that seemed unlikely and a black belt in judo, so no one argued with her too much. KC liked her and found her enquiring mind often set going a train of new ideas he had not considered.

Julia was seated at her desk when he entered.

'Hi KC, come to talk toasters, I believe.'

'Yes, tell me about them.'

He sat comfortably in the other chair.

'Right, what we did was talked to the manufacturer about the assembly process. They checked all the adjacent batches, and none showed up with this problem. It's a standard item, and there are no reports of any other accidents from a similar defect. In fact, the only other fatality this year was a fire started by a toaster placed within two inches of net curtains. The wind blew the curtains onto the heating element and poof! They never learn.'

'So toasters. These days are made of heat resistant and flame retardant moulded plastic, as this one was. The electrical cord is threaded into the plastic base, and all the wire bits are added. Then the body of the toaster is fitted over the base. So, to get a bare wire at the point where the cable enters the base means you have to pare back the outer sheath of the cable or melt it, say a quick stab with a soldering iron. You can't just pull it. The chances of this happening during manufacturing are very low. Toasters are tested on the assembly line.'

'You mean they make toast?'

'Sure. There is one company who makes so much toast they donate it to local farmers who use it as livestock feed. So, my line of thinking is that is unlikely that the company was at fault. The odds are against this. So, the damage occurred at the base of the toaster. It was either a case of someone doing something very stupid, like tampering with the cable to make it longer or shorter. Or someone has deliberately damaged the plastic covering and exposed the metal wires. But we can't tell which. Let me show you.'

Julia let him to a work bench where the disassembled toaster lay like a skeleton.

'Now look here. This is the cable. As you can see, it melted with the heat of the electrical charge, as did most of the victim's fingers. The plastic sheathing is just a blob. There is no way I can tell what it looked like before the accident.'

She held up the cable so KC could look closely, then waggled it in front of him.

'Sorry. There is no way to tell. All I can give you are the odds of this being deliberate, which I would say is fifty-fifty, and that won't stand up in court. We have looked at every inch of this toaster and apart from a few unidentifiable smudges and those prints from the victim, there is no sign anyone else had touched it. Not strange as they polish them over at the end of the assembly line before packing, and the workers wear cloth gloves to keep smears off the shiny bodywork.'

'Right, then, motive and opportunity,' KC was thinking allowed as he often did when he was with Julia.

'Who handled the toaster? When it was collected, the box was sealed with tape. That is, we think it was. We are looking through CCTV from the store to see if we can find an image of the toaster being collected. Who handled the toaster then? So, the list is Mak Mason, maybe Pattie Harding. I will ask her. Then Aunt Maud who conveniently dies. Then Mak again, then Janis, maybe her brother, then finally Delia Mason.'

'That is a long chain of possible suspects. All in the same family, so all would gain either directly or indirectly from this death, but not substantially, except for Mak. If the toaster was prepared to kill Aunt Maud, then it was tampered with before Mak delivered it to his Aunt, that implicates only Mak and Pattie. If it was tampered with after Aunt Maud's death to kill Delia specifically, then we have to add Janis and Joe to the list.'

'I am afraid, KC, you have too many ifs, no strong motives and no conclusive evidence. This looks like a case of an accidental death. The shop says that the toaster was unopened when sold, i.e. it was not a returned product. I think you need the CCTV of the sale. That might show that the box was sealed when Mak collected it and would rule out the store's negligence.

KC sighed. Two deaths in one family in a short space of time is unusual, but not impossible. Was it improbable? He stood on his toes and smiled up at Julia and mouthed 'thanks, beautiful', then retreated before she tried a judo move on him. He walked quickly back to this own building, thinking of the attractive forensic scientist. Sadly, she was just too tall for him and chopping off her feet was not an option. He chuckled to himself for his politically incorrect thoughts as he climbed the stairs.

Later that day, the team assembled, as instructed, to review the findings. The financial checks were ongoing. The banks saw no need to hurry and anyway they had few staff these days, and this type of requests was an annoyance. The rechecked statements threw up nothing new and the statements from the neighbours were not helpful. Nor was local area CCTV.

The store had provided a grainy but visible film of Mak collecting the toaster. Only Mak could be seen at the counter, so Pattie may not have been with him or was out of the shot. The camera was placed above the customer to the right side of the counter, looking down, so the items and the transaction could be seen. The assistant placed the box on the counter to one side and then completed the transaction. The box was sealed. There was no doubt about it. Mak's face was clearly visible as he turned and left the counter and faced the camera.

'Well done,' said KC. 'I would like most of you to move onto the other jobs in hand. Once we get the financial picture, we will see who we need to interview next. For now, I think we must assume this is an accidental death and prepare all the paperwork for the coroner. Tomorrow is another day, people.'

———

WEDNESDAY 1 MARCH

No amount of speculation was going to make the case any clearer. KC arrived early the next day. He needed new evidence, or this one would go to the coroner the following week as an accidental death, an unsolved case to be sealed in a file in the registry, with the boxes of evidence tucked away for a specified number of years in case something came up.

As there was no actual hard evidence that this was any more than an accident, KC thought he might just try nudging Mak a bit and see what happened. He needed to separate him from Pattie before he tried that, or he would get nothing. Mak would hide behind Pattie or she would come out with guns blazing to protect her man. If only, he thought and sighed. He called Mak's phone.

'Mak's phone. You can leave a message with me.'

'Good morning, Pattie. I would like a word with Mak, please.'

There was a silence as Pattie realised by his voice that KC was very serious, and this was official.

'Okay, fetching him for you.'

He heard her walk through the flat and open a door; the bedroom he expected.

'For you, it's KC.'

He could hear the phone being handed over and a door close in the distance.

'Hello Mak, how are you today?'

Mak grunted.

'I would like to talk to you today. We are hoping to present the evidence of your wife's death to the Coroner's Court next week. The hearing is set for Tuesday the fourteenth, by the way. You don't have to be there, but I am sure Janis and Joe will want your support, you being their Dad. So, if you could come into the station today, say about two this afternoon, we will just dot the i's, etc. I won't need to talk to Pattie, so no need for her to come out in the cold.'

It was a pathetic excuse, and Mak would know it. KC wanted to talk to Mak alone, and there would be no arguments. Mak sighed.

'Right see you at two then and Pattie can keep warm, can't she.'

KC heard the mobile click off. So far so good. Now he must think of some questions.

Mak got up and rubbed his hands through his hair. It was getting long again. 'Good', he thought. He stared hard into the mirror as he shaved. He felt like he was standing outside of his body, like a ghost, looking at someone he once knew. He wanted to go and play his music for an hour or two, listen to songs for the next set, try to get a grip on reality. He put his laptop on and played through some of the songs he had picked for the next bingo set. The prophetic lyrics of Chris Rea's 'Road to Hell' made him stop and listen. He picked up his guitar and strummed along. Maybe do a cover of this on Saturday night. The others would pick it up quick, and he was the only one who needed to remember the words, anyway. He turned as Pattie came in.

'Thought we should do this, hun. What do you think? Suits my voice, eh?'

Pattie nodded and waited, looking hard at him. He looked back but knew he had to explain to her sooner or later.

'Police want to talk to me before they send the papers to the coroner. KC was most concerned that you should stay indoors out of the cold. Nice of him, you think?'

'You mean he wants to talk to you without me being there?'

'Yep, you got it.' He looked at her helplessly.

'I am sure you will cope, Mak. Big boy now.'

Mal looked as if he was not sure that he would cope, as Pattie came close and studied his eyes intently. She took his face between her hands, caressing the newly shaved skin. She loved this man and whatever it cost her, that would not change. She rubbed his nose with hers and they both smiled, sharing a moment of closeness. Mak's tired eyes showed tiny flecks of orange around the dark pupils. That inner fire was still burning.

Pattie let him go and went through to the kitchen. Mak would have to face this alone. That was what KC had in mind. But why? Could it be possible that he suspected Mak of harming Delia? That was unthinkable. Delia was unbearable at times, but not so unbearable that anyone would kill her. She would not speculate. Her whole life centered on her relationship with Mak. A mistake in retrospect to let so much of her future depend on one man. She knew what she had done. If she had done things differently, there would be no Mak, and she could not bear that thought. Listening to him play, hearing him talk, was a drug she could not give up, not now, not ever.

Mak came into the kitchen dressed and ready to face the interview. He looked so tired. He had tried to talk with Janis and Joe, but so far the three had sat in silence eating pizza. Everything had come to a stop. Nothing was moving forward, and the past would not come back. Delia was dead, and they could not even bury her. Her noisy, infuriating ghost hung over everything. She would not go easy or quietly.

'I'll drive you, then do some shopping. You can call me when you want to be collected. How's that?'

She came close and ruffled his hair. Mak looked at her as if he wanted to say something. There was an urgency in his eyes that she did not understand.

'Okay, sounds like a plan. Is it cold out?'

'Yes, darling, it is cold now till spring.'

They put on their warmest coats and scarfs and went down the stairs to the car.

Mak was kept waiting. He arrived and asked for KC, then was shown into a bare interview room. His fingerprints were taken and then the constable brought him a luke-warm cup of coffee. Mak sat slumped in the chair, occasionally drumming on the table with his fingers. He had seen this on TV; there were hidden cameras and KC was watching him. He was sure of that. KC was at that moment sitting at his desk chewing a pencil as he thought about how he might proceed with the interview. Mak was not a fool, so he would lay his evidence firmly on the table and see what came back.

KC greeted Mak formally.

'I am sorry about your wife's death. At this stage, we are still investigating what happened.'

Mak nodded. He planned to say as little as possible.

'We can now say conclusively that she died from electrocution by touching an exposed wire on the toaster that you brought her. So, my job is to investigate the life of the toaster, so to speak, see where it has been up to the moment when it killed your wife.'

He opened an iPad and placed it in front of Mak.

'Let's watch the movie, shall we? Now you can see. Here you are collecting the toaster from Argos. The box is sealed and when we pan in we can see that the tape is nice and crisp and new. The store's merchandising computer tells us that the toaster was recently delivered to the warehouse and had not been a returned product, as they are known. So here you are receiving a pristine new red toaster for your Aunt. Was Pattie with you on that day?'

'I think she was in the car or she went to do some other shopping while I collected it.'

'Okay, so next step is you delivering the toaster to your Aunt. When you got home, did you leave it in the car, or did you take it to the flat?'

'We took it indoors, and it was on the hall table for a couple of days. Then I took it round to Maud's on the Tuesday before she died, if I recall right.'

'So when you delivered it, did you go in and have coffee, maybe set it up for her?'

'Naw, my Aunt was quite capable of taking a toaster out of a box. I went in, put it on her kitchen table, I think. She made me a coffee; we chatted a bit, and then I went to band practise.'

'So she didn't open the toaster while you were there?'

'Nope, we talked about her new gas boiler. The house was like an oven. I didn't stay too long.'

'So she liked her place warm then. Maybe explains why she opened the patio doors on the night she died.'

Mak nodded.

'So after she died, you took the toaster back to your place again.'

'I took some jewellery, family photographs, a small TV and the toaster. I was gonna take it back, but Maud had paid for it online, so that was too much trouble. Then I thought I would give it to Dearest.'

'Why did you think that?'

'She liked red things, red fridge, red kettle, etc. I thought it might improve her mood a bit. She was being unreasonable over the divorce.'

'So the toaster was on your hall table for about a month, and the box was not sealed, right?'

'Aunt Maud had sliced open the tape, looked inside, but

not unpacked it. So, when I took it over to Janis, I re-taped the top of the box to make it easier to carry.'

'So anyone in your place could have opened the box and took the toaster out and then repacked it.'

'Yea, but we got better things to do.' Mak was irritated.

'So you resealed the box and took it to your daughter's so she could give to her mother. Why didn't you just deliver it to your wife's place or her salon?'

'I was trying to keep my distance from Dearest. She's not, was not, taking the divorce too kindly. Seemed better somehow if Janis gave it to her. Janis ain't stupid. She knew the divorce was happening, however much her mother screamed about it.'

'So the toaster was delivered to Janis on the day when you showed the estate agent around the house. How did the kids feel about that?'

'Janis was moving in with Dearest, and Joe didn't give a fuck. I need to square things. I am in debt, badly in debt.'

'We know,' said KC.

There was a moment while Mak considered what might have been happening. It was clear that the police had looked at his money problems in detail and there was not a lot he could do about that. His face felt hot, but there was no reason to show he was angry.

'Yea, cos you do. Been digging around in my life. Could have asked me. I got nothing to hide. I would have told you.'

'Of course. Now Janis held onto the toaster for a few days and then dropped it over to her mother's. Is that your under-standing?'

'Dearest came flying over when she saw the toaster. Must have been a Sunday evening, the day after the Leopard gig. I remember cos the landlord was talking about cutting down on our sets and getting another band to do alternate weeks. Guys were not happy at first; they got used to the regular money. So have I.'

'That's a shame, Mak.'

'Yea, pissed me off. So, then Dearest barges in and starts going on about the divorce and how she didn't need a toaster. She could be nasty sometimes. She upsets Pattie.'

'I dare say. So as far as you can tell us, you collected the toaster from the store, took it home, before taking it to your Aunt. Then collected it and took it home, sealed it and delivered it to your daughter's place. Janis took it to her mother's house.'

'Right.' Mak sighed.

'So apart from adding an extra strip of tape to the top of the box, you never removed the contents or repacked them?'

'Right. Are you suggesting something here? I am sorry Dearest is dead. Now I got the hassle of helping my kids bury their mother. She was a pain, a real pain at times, but after ten years, it doesn't seem unreasonable to get a divorce, does it?'

'I can't say, Mak. I have never been married.'

'Well, you should try it sometimes. You get the wrong woman, and it can all go pear-shaped and before you know it, you are just a money machine. It's money for this and money for that. It never stops.'

'I think perhaps most women are different these days, Mak. I'm sure Pattie is good with money.'

Mak took a deep breath. KC was winding him up.

'Leave Pattie out of this. She did the accounts for Dearest, but that was a business arrangement. She tried to stay as far away from Dearest as she could. They didn't like each other. Why should they? But I was with Pattie, whether Dearest liked it or not, and Pattie kept her nose out of my family affairs.'

'And you would do anything for Pattie, right?'

'That does not come into it. Pattie never asks me for anything. She runs her own business and helps me out a lot. She is a clever woman. She could more than handle Dearest when she needed to.'

The interview was going nowhere. Mak was sullen but was sticking to the facts. There was nothing to be gained by pushing him any further. KC stood up and collected his iPad and papers.

'Thanks, Mak, for coming in. I am going to be in touch with Janis and Joe as soon as we can release the body for burial. I assume you will help the kids with the arrangements. Your wife has left no will, so I guess everything is divided equally between the children. The house, of course, is yours. I understand you are not selling their house for the time being.'

Mak nodded.

'As soon as this is sorted, I will sell the houses and give the kid's their share; then they will be set up.'

'Generous of you, Mak, but only what the court would give them, I expect. Thanks for your time.'

KC went back to his desk with a lot to think about. There were no flaws or inconsistencies in Mak's statement. They were simply two men who did not like each other. Phones were ringing, and there was a lot of noise and chatter and finally he looked up from his notes and waited for someone to tell him what was going on.

'Clowns,' said the sergeant. 'Local school had a visiting theatre group, and in the play, there was a clown. All the kids started screaming and running home. Parents are calling us to complain. Plain daft if you ask me.'

KC shook his head. Media overreaction was the order of the day. Plain daft was right. Whatever are we teaching our kids, he wondered? Time to prepared his report for the coroner's court. He would have to talk to Janis and Joe before the report was final, but it seemed like an accident. Maybe Delia decided to modify the toaster cable herself and forgot to turn it off. Maybe he would never know. His instincts told him one thing, and the evidence told him another.

———

THURSDAY 9 MARCH

There was some early spring sunshine for Delia Mason's funeral. Janis had proved herself very capable and made all the arrangements. She hoped her mother would have liked the enormous quantity of flowers and wicker basket coffin. There would be a wreath spelling out 'Dearest' on top of the coffin. The salon had been closed since her Delia's death, and Paulina had taken a month's wages and found a job in another salon, where she might finally get some proper training.

Janis had decided not to take up the lease, and Pattie was finalising the books so the business could be closed. Janis had ideas about a nail salon in Spain. She saw no reason to stick around. She missed her mother but was secretly enjoying the sudden responsibility her mother's death had given her. Joe was silent and pale. He slept most of the time.

As the Coroner's hearing was set for the next Tuesday, so KC arranged to interview the siblings on the day before the funeral. He arrived early to find Janis on the phone, inviting people to attend the next day. It was to be a Royal Command funeral. She made him coffee in the kitchen and then called her brother to get up and come downstairs. Joe arrived wearing a tracksuit, which he looked to have slept in. His hair was a mess, and his eyes were red-rimmed. He slumped in a chair, and Janis made his coffee.

'Now I am sorry to call today, as I know it is a busy time for you both. There are some questions that I should answer before I send my final report to the coroner. We believe your mother's death was accidental. We don't really know how, but we think she somehow put her wet fingers on a bare wire underneath the toaster. Death was instant. She didn't suffer.'

He looked at Janis, expecting her to be tearful. She was not, but Joe looked like he might cry at any minute.

'Now, for the record, we need to check the movements of this toaster. You say that your father brought it to you on the day the estate agent called to value the house?'

Janis nodded.

'Was the box sealed?'

'Yes. Dad had brought it from Aunt Maud's. She never used it, poor thing.'

'So the box was sealed and was here for a few days before you took it to your mother's place. Is that right?'

'Mum and Dad were arguing about the divorce. Mum did not understand that she had no choice. I tried to convince her that it was a good thing, make an end, and move on and so on. But she wasn't having any of it, so the toaster was here for that week. She had been ringing Dad every day and every time she got Pattie, who just said she would get Dad to call her. Of course, he didn't.'

I took the toaster over the Sunday before she died. I was waiting until it was a nice morning and she was at home. Dad thought it might make her better tempered. As usual, it made things worse. She went round to their flat, and there was a hell of a fight, I heard.'

'Did she open the box when you were there?'

'No, she just left it on the table. She said it made her feel sick. Said she was being pacified with a toaster, she said. Being bought. That was how she saw it.'

KC wondered how anyone could be pacified with a toaster. In this case, silenced maybe.

'So while the toaster was here, did you, or you Joe, open the box, say to look at it?'

'No,' snapped Janis, getting quite angry.

'Why the fuck would I look at a toaster?' Joe replied. 'My mum is dead, and you don't seem to be finding out why.'

He wiped his eyes with his sleeve. Joe's world was just falling apart, and he was feeling new emotions that he was embarrassed and ashamed of. His mother had been a cow sometimes, but he loved her, and now he was feeling things he had never expected to feel. He sniffed.

'Joe, we are pretty sure your mother's death was an accident, but that is up to the coroner to decide that, not me. I just collect all the facts.'

They sat in silence until Janis offered more coffee, which KC declined.

'I will be at the funeral tomorrow if that is alright with you both. Pay my respects to your mum and so on.'

Neither objected.

Janis had ordered two cars to take herself, Joe, Paulina and some of their cousins to the crematorium. Mak arrived with Pattie in his battered car just as the hearse arrived at the house. The party would follow the funeral car to the crematorium. Everyone looked much as they had done on the day of Aunt Maud's funeral, except for Janis. She was wearing her mother's coat with the big collar. The shock of her mother's death had changed her, and she looked confident and stronger. She had come out from her mother's shadow at last. Joe looked tired and was probably a bit stoned. He didn't wear his bright green gloves.

The cars moved off slowly in procession. A few neighbours stood in the street. All the curtains were closed in an old-fashioned mark of respect for the dead. Even the Indian family stood outside to watch them pass. It was a good neighbourhood. People came from everywhere, all peaceful families, all feeling the tragedy on their doorstep. A few streets further on, the cars drove past the salon with the blinds closed and a black edged notice pasted in the window announcing the death of the owner, Mrs Delia Mason. There was only one spelling mistake, but no one was likely to notice. Around the next corner, there was an unusual sight. Paulina gave a little shriek of surprise as they drove past a clown standing alone in a small patch of wasteland. He was not scary, not to an adult; a sort of clown meets Clockwork Orange character. He wore a homemade mask and an orange wig, with a bowler hat perched on the top. The rest of him was dressed normally in jeans and a t-shirt with a white sheet draped over his shoulders. As the procession passed, he removed his hat in an elaborate bow, like a courtier at a palace ball.

'What the fuck,' Joe said. 'Is that a Pokémon thingy?'

No one answered. Joe would work it out, eventually.

Following in the old Jaguar, Mak looked at Pattie and shrugged.

'At least he is respectful. You gotta love that clown hair,' he said, and they both laughed.

The chapel was full, and it was clear that Janis had planned her mother's funeral very well. There were wreaths and bouquets piled high. A large framed photo of Delia in a red party dress was set on the coffin. She was very pretty once. Neighbours and clients had put on their finest for the occasion, and there was a festive air like it was a saint's feast day. Mak and Pattie sat behind Janis and Joe and the assorted cousins. A few nodded to him in acknowledgement, but none spoke. Arriving late, KC sat in the last row and observed the crowd. He had only met Delia Mason once, but he thought she would enjoy the theatricality of the event. He was certain she would not enjoy being dead. The woman had the ability to cling firmly to life as she had tried to cling on to her husband. He saw Mak's shoulder's tighten as another cringe-worthy eighties tune filled the chapel. Depeche Mode and Wham seemed quite in keeping with the tone of the day. The coffin trundled on its way to the sound of Spandau Ballet's song 'True'. KC reminded himself to write in his will, 'No funeral please.'

After it was all over, Janis stood by the pile of wreaths, thanking everyone. She was rising to the occasion. She hugged Mak and briefly smiled at Pattie. Joe had disappeared for a cigarette among the memorial rose trees.

'You still thinking of Spain?' Mak asked.

'Yea. Thinking I will go. This country is finished and there's a maniac in the White House now, so it's time I got away. I think Joe and I are pretty much sorted. Thanks, Dad.'

She seemed cold and detached, like she was giving a performance. Mak was reminded of how much she resembled her mother, but it might be because she was wearing her coat. He was not sure how Donald Trump's election was likely to influence his daughter's career in the beauty industry.

Pattie wandered ahead and found KC standing by the cars with his hands deep in his pockets and shivering in the wind. She guessed he was waiting for her.

'Sad day. I had to come and pay my respects.'

'Checking for someone to pin a murder on, are you?'

'No. Accidental death, or so I expect the coroner will decide next week. We have no evidence of anything else.'

They were quiet and walked slowly along between the damp aisles of shrubs.

'I wanted to ask you a question, if I may?'

'Go on. You could arrest me and interrogate me, but if it's only one question, you better ask now and save me a trip.'

'When Mak collected the toaster, you didn't go into the store. You waited for him in the car?'

'That's right.'

'Then the toaster stood on your hall table for a couple of weeks until Mak took it to his Aunt's.'

'About right. I put it in the cupboard.'

'So, he took it back to your place. Was the box opened or sealed?'

'The top of the box was opened. There was a lot going on at that time. I didn't have time to go tampering with a toaster, if that is what you are asking me. Mak sealed it before he delivered it to Janis. He got the tape from my desk drawer. I know because he left the tape out on the desk.'

It was beginning to drizzle, and they turned and walked back to the cars.

'Got what you want, Detective Inspector?'

Pattie stopped and faced him. Her lips were red with the cold. KC wanted to kiss them.

'Thanks, Pattie. I have everything for my report now.'

She looked at him cynically and seeing Mak waiting by the car; she walked towards him without saying goodbye.'

'What did he want?' asked Mak suspiciously as they got in the car.

'Nothing important, Mak, forget it.'

———

TUESDAY 14 MARCH

The same group of people assembled a few days later for the inquest. Everyone was wearing much the same clothes. It was the time of year where people just wrapped up warm; all tired and fed-up with the long winter. The bleak weather mirrored exactly the bleak future the misinformed voters of Britain had carved out for themselves. Some people were leaving, and others were making plans. Many were searching around for an Irish ancestor so they could apply for a second passport. Australia and Canada were looking forward to welcoming an influx of doctors, nurses and teachers. Britain's loss would be the former colonies' gain. Mak and Pattie had briefly discussed moving to Portugal, but their plans were still vague.

KC arrived smartly dressed for his appearance before the court. Beside him was Julia Winterton, the very tall forensic officer, who would also report her findings to the coroner. Everyone trooped into the overheated courtroom. The chairs were hard, but no one was staying any longer than necessary. The doctor's report was read out by the court official. Death by electrocution causing a cardiac seizure.

Next KC gave his report. He took the witness stand briskly and confidently, then opened his notebook. His report was equally brisk, giving just the facts, formally and concisely. He looked towards Janis and commended her prompt action in calling the police and ambulance. Janis looked pleased and straightened in her seat so all could see her.

Julia Winterton was next. Her report was technical, and no one listened; they were too busy looking at her beautiful twist braided hair. Her report concluded that death was caused by the victim touching an exposed wire on the base of the toaster, but she had no way of showing how the wire had come to be exposed. There was no evidence that the manufacturer was at fault or that the toaster was tampered with at the store or after. No conclusion could be drawn.

The Coroner took little time in pronouncing a verdict of accidental death. There was a feeling of anti-climax as everyone moved back into the hallway. Pattie looked around for KC, but he was leaving with the tall forensic officer; they were both smiling and talking. Pattie felt that this was just another job to them, and they were moving onto the next. Mak was talking to Janis. Pattie walked over to Joe, who looked in need of comfort.

'How are you, Joe?'

She looked at his red eyes and unhealthy skin. She was trying to work out if it was grief, guilt or drugs.

'All right, thanks for asking,' Joe said in a husky voice.

'Anything we can do, Joe?' she asked.

'Nope. Just miss me, Mum, that's all. She didn't need to die like that.'

'I'm sorry Joe, I really am.'

Joe looked at her. He had no reason to dislike Pattie. None of this was her fault. He was just looking for someone to blame, and he couldn't find anyone. He was feeling helpless and impotent.

'Well, like I said, anything we can do. Come to your Dad's set on Saturday week. Rest of the band are retiring. He's doing a solo gig, so I think you will enjoy it.'

'Maybe. Thanks, Pattie.'

He hunched into his hoodie and hunted in his pocket for the bright green gloves. The fingers were torn and nicotine stained. Pattie watched him go. She didn't want to speculate on Joe's future. She knew Mak planned to share the money from Dearest's house with the kids. She hoped Janis would be content with that and not get greedy like her mother. Joe's share would probably go right up in smoke.

Mak came over and put his arm through hers.

'Let's go home, darlin'. I am cold and tired. Got work to do as well. Saturday is only a week away, and I still have to learn ten more songs.'

———

MONDAY 20 MARCH

Mak knew the day had to come, eventually. The rest of the band had other lives and other jobs. They had already made backing tracks for the times when Marilyn made so much fuss that Peter thought it not worth the argument to show up. Mick was going deaf and the day when he could no longer play was getting closer. The landlord of the Leopard thought it was time for a change and had suggested another younger band should play every other week. Instead, Mak offered to play a solo set on three Saturdays each month. If the other members were available, then they could come along and sit in. The landlord was shrewd, and he knew Mak was the one the audience came for. So, a deal was struck. The rest of the band seemed relieved. Their time was over, and they accepted it.

Mak already had the backing tracks he needed. He got some new songs and the other band members recorded parts for him. The tracks were loaded onto his computer. Now all he needed was the energy to front a solo show all by himself. Pattie listened from her office all week while he rehearsed. The flats were empty during the day as most people were out at work, so there was no one to complain about the noise.

Mak had put three layers of carpet on the floor of his

music room. It helped deaden the sound, and there were few complaints. Mak was too good for that. The neighbours simply turned their radios off and enjoyed the music. Pattie had typed and printed out the playlist, and now she listened without comment while he rehearsed. He certainly was a perfectionist, as far as his music was concerned. The other areas of his life were far more chaotic. Pattie often wondered what would happen if there was ever a day when Mak could not play. She imagined it was like having wings and not being able to fly. His pain would be awful.

Finally, he invited her in to hear the full set. She armed herself with a notepad and sat quietly in the armchair and made notes as he played. They discussed her comments over the dinner.

'So, am I ready to go alone?' Mak asked.

'I think so. You got your work cut out finding new material, but maybe you can cover more of the tunes you play at the bingo. They seem to like what you play there.'

Mak thought about this and then reached over the table and took her hand.

'I'm sorry about all this.'

'Not your fault, Mak. You didn't murder them. It has just been a series of unfortunate accidents. These things happen. It's your Joe that worries me most now.'

'Yes. I noticed. But what do we do? My boy takes after me. He doesn't like taking advice, we know that.'

'I think we could give him a meal occasionally. Invite him to the Leopard when you play solo. Say you need his help or something like that.'

'Yes, perhaps. And perhaps he'll come and perhaps he won't.'

'But we can ask, Mak. That's all we can do.'

They sat quietly, sipping their wine and watching the lights come on in the block opposite as people arrived home and settled down after a day's hard work. The evenings had started to pull out, and there was still a faint glow of daylight behind the tall towers. Spring was on its way. In the country-side, there would be spring flowers and newborn lambs; in the city, the stark concrete would be brightened by rays of sunlight.

Brexit was biting, and no one knew if there would be a future for the country or if it would become just a holiday destination for historical tourism. A country of ancient castles, Downton Abbey and Agatha Christie novels. Pattie was determined they should leave and soon, before the bleakness was total and the landscape blighted by pollution and unen-durable sadness.

KC was having very similar thoughts as he settled down to lead his team through the latest investigation of a series of burglaries on the industrial estate. Small scale thefts with small profits, but costly to the business owners, who had to replace doors and windows and fit new locks and alarms. It was slow, painstaking work with a small mountain of forensic evidence to shift through and analyse. His trips to the 'Super-model' were frequent. Her laboratory was clear of toasters and packing boxes and now full of glass fragments and broken locks and battered alarms. He seated himself comfort-ably in her office. He could have just telephoned, but he liked to get out of the office, and he did his most productive thinking when he had an intelligent colleague to bounce his ideas off. Then, out of the blue, Julia mentioned the two deaths.

'You know, KC, I am still very unsure about that toaster.'

'In what way?'

'Well, all the prints were Delia Mason's, except for a couple of unexplained smudges. They were not finger prints as such, but I have begun to think that they could be glove prints.'

'Explain, please.'

'Well, glove prints can be simple marks left by the seams

or folds in the fabric of a glove. Or they can be complex, like marks left behind by the grain or texture of the fabric of a glove. We can now collect and analyse any prints left at a crime scene that were created by someone wearing gloves. Here we have two small smudges on the base of the toaster that could be made by someone wearing gloves.'

'Or?'

'Or they could be made by the packers on the assembly line. They normally wear cloth gloves which they use to polish the surface at the same time. These marks look like surgical gloves and anyone with half a brain would know that prints can be obtained this way, so would have worn two pairs and polished the surface afterwards. Perhaps someone unpacked the toaster and touched the cable with a soldering iron and melted back the outer casing or took a sharp knife and pared it back. Because of the melted remains, we can't tell if this happened.'

KC looked interested. He stretched his arms out wide as he considered this information.

'So you are saying that there is a possibility that the death of Delia Mason was murder?'

'I am saying that there is a possibility, but one that I cannot prove forensically. Even if we had the gloves he wore, I don't think we have much chance of proving it. And those gloves would be long gone. If this is a crime, it is a well-executed crime, and we won't find any traces.'

'So, my lady of the dark arts, you are suggesting that Mak Mason tampered with that toaster before he delivered it to his Aunt.'

'I am suggesting, KC, that Mak is the one with the strongest motive and the nimblest fingers.'

'So it might have been that Mak wanted to kill his Aunt for her assets, but she conveniently killed herself. So, he simply passed the murder weapon on to his wife to put an end to her increasing demands and speed up the sale of the house, which she could have delayed for months, even years.

Money from those houses will cover his debts. It does not seem possible that a man with his God-given gift would risk everything. His finances are in a mess, that was true, and it is likely the tax man is after him, too. Still hard to believe and he is the only possible suspect, with motive and opportunity. He can be abrupt and surly. I don't think he likes me very much, but I can't see him as a murderer.'

KC was thinking of Pattie at that moment.

'Well, it crossed my mind, so I mentioned it. Bring me the gloves and I might be able to prove it, or I might not. It is all too speculative.'

'I am afraid so. I have the high-ups on my back about these burglaries. No sense in making more work, for either of us, even if we had the resources to see it through.'

They both sighed and got back to discussing the more urgent crimes. But the idea lay at the back of KC's mind like a dog waiting to leap on an intruder.

————

SATURDAY 25 MARCH

K C saw the poster for Mak's solo debut pinned up in the kebab shop. He wanted to go along but thought he had outstayed his welcome the last time. Best stay away. He was crossing the town around mid-morning and would pass by the Leopard, so it occurred to him that he could legitimately drop by and see if there was a sound check in progress. At least he could hear a little of the set and grab a sandwich and coffee at the bar. He parked in the pub carpark and started to walk over to the back entrance when Pattie came out. She had dropped Mak off with his equipment and now would do her shopping until Mak was ready to leave for home. She stopped and looked at him, not exactly sure what to say. KC came over and asked how they were.

'Mak is fine, thanks.' She hesitated, unsure of how much she should say to him. After all that had happened, she wanted to keep away from this man. He disrupted her thoughts. KC smiled encouragingly and noticed her shiver in the cold wind.

'Let me buy you a coffee,' he suggested and steered her out of the wind into the laneway beside the pub and into the welcoming coffee shop at the end. He fetched two coffees and pastries and settled down opposite her. Her skin shone from the cold, and she pulled her hair loose from her beret and ran her fingers through it. She was unsure of him but curious as to why he was always so keen to talk to her.

'So Janis is going to Spain next month,' she said. 'Joe is still a bit subdued, but then that is to be expected, poor kid. He's coming to his Dad's gig tonight, which is a first.'

She sipped her coffee and waited for him to explain why he was there.

'Well, wish Mak the best of luck. I am sure he will be excellent. It's about time he went solo. He is still a real talent.'

'Yes, he is.'

Her voice was soft and very gentle. He wondered if it was love in Pattie's voice when she spoke about Mak. He wanted very much for a woman to speak of him with such warmth and admiration.

'And how is the house sale working out? Got any offers yet?'

'One, I believe. Early days yet. Look KC, why am I here? What is it you want? I am sorry about Delia, but it was an accident. It's the kids we should be concerned for now. And Mak, he was shocked too. You can't be married to someone for years and not feel pain when something like this happens to them, even if the marriage didn't work out.'

KC stared into his coffee cup. He was unsure how to go on, and he hesitated just long enough for Pattie to have doubts.

'Are you suggesting that something is not right here? The coroner gave his verdict. Accidental death, that's what he said. Right? The case is closed.'

Pattie was looking at him, trying to detect something in his words that he was not saying out loud. She drank her coffee and waited. KC knew he should not suggest it, but she was bright enough to know that something was on his mind.

'You know, Pattie, the coroner gave his judgement based

on the evidence presented to him. We have no evidence that Delia's death was other than a tragic accident.'

Pattie was already pulling on her coat and hat.

'Don't do this, KC. I know what you are suggesting, and you can stop it right now. Mak would never, ever hurt anyone, especially Delia. She was a pain, but that was all. He would not harm his kid's mother. I know what you are playing at, and you can back off, do you hear?'

She grabbed her purse and threw a five-pound note in his face. Then, with a furious look, she left the café. He watched her struggle into her coat as she braced herself against the wind. Her hair was flying around her eyes; he could see the loose strands of gold and silver whirling around. Finally, she trapped them, and wound the unruly hair furiously into a knot and tucked it inside her beret. Then she turned a corner and was gone from his view.

KC sat alone and drank his coffee, realising he had given himself away. Women always knew when they were wanted, when they were desired. They had a nose for it, a built-in detection device. No amount of denials would convince Pattie that his interest in Mak was not contaminated by his desire for her. He was not sure himself. Pattie believed so strongly that Mak was incapable of killing his wife. Perhaps he should trust her judgement and let it go. He could be wrong.

Pattie did her shopping and then collected Mak. He looked pleased and excited. She asked him if the sound check had gone okay and how he was feeling.

'Tired and nervous but let me sleep for the rest of the afternoon, and I shall be ready for anything.'

He leant across and kissed her. Both could feel the old thrill.

While he slept, Pattie lay in the bath and tried to wash away the stain of her conversation with KC. He was just winding her up because he fancied her. She should report

143

him, but she thought better of it. Best to say nothing and not allow his petty jealously to push a wedge between her and Mak. She believed in Mak. He could not have tampered with that toaster. He would not do such a thing. She knew him. She loved him. And yet there were some things she did not know. The porn site, for instance. She did not know about that. She had been shocked, but more saddened than angry. Men were strange creatures; they never grow up really. Mak was behaving just like Joe probably behaved. She would say nothing about it.

She thought back to the days when the red toaster had sat on the hall table. Mak had brought it from his Aunt's, and there it sat until he took it round to Janis. She saw no sign of him unpacking it or touching it. He never paid any attention to it. He had resealed the box flaps and delivered it round to his daughter. No, it was impossible. KC was just trying to make her doubt Mak, that was all.

She thought about their future. The two houses would sell, and that should make a sizable dent in Mak's debts. He was letting Joe stay in the other house after Janis left for Spain. He thought Joe could be encouraged to move into a smaller place or with one of his mates once his sister had left. Then that house could be sold too. And then what? If the show went well tonight, Mak might want to try to reboot his career. It was not something she could push him into. He would know if that was the right way to go. She would go along with him, whatever he did. With Delia's death, she had lost one of her clients, so perhaps it was time to give up her small-scale booking keeping and look for something more challenging. There was a lot riding on that night's show.

She dressed carefully. Her usual black draped trousers and a blouse with a tie at the neck. She stared at herself in the mirror. Her youth had gone. There were lines around her mouth now, and her neck had lost some of its tone. She regretted the passing of the years and wondered if she could have filled them better. Loving Mak had turned out to be hard work, but she had always known it would be. Standing beside him made her happier than anything in the world. When Mak woke up, she made him some tea and an omelette. They would eat dinner later. He got ready and then presented himself for her inspection.

'Geez, you are a looker, Makenzie Mason, you know that?'

Mak grinned. He had a new black shirt and wore his cowboy boots from his rock and roll days. At least playing solo meant he could sit down for most of the numbers. He had lost weight in the last three months. Pattie stood on her toes for a kiss.

'Don't you distract me, you groupie. I've got to concentrate tonight.'

'You will be great, Mak. I know you will.'

And he was. The pub was packed. There was the usual crowd, plus those who wanted to see if Mak Mason could pull this one off. Mick, the deaf drummer, came along with his wife, and Joe arrived just before the start and disappeared outside with Mak for the usual smoke. Father and son came back into the pub together, and Joe stood chatting to Mak while he settled on stage. Joe picked up the acoustic guitar and strummed a few chords. Maybe Joe could play after all. Pattie watched from a table at one side until Joe came and sat beside her and grinned at her.

The tables were filling up, and in the restaurant, families were tucking into scampi and burgers. Everything came with chips. When it was time, the landlord's son quickly adjusted the microphone and Mak began to play.

It is hard to define that mystical quality they call stage presence. Some people have it, and some don't. It often disguises a lack of real talent, when the mediocre is hidden behind the well-rehearsed presence of a slick performer. That night, Mak had both stage presence and talent. He played well; some would say brilliantly, as well as Jimmy Page or

145

Eric Clapton, but he also had that magical quality that made you want to look at him.

The audience sang along, danced occasionally, but mostly just watched and listened and enjoyed. He played the songs of their teenage years, the songs of their first love and their last. He played the songs of heartbreak and loneliness, all the songs they knew and remembered. He played for two hours without a break and at the end, no one wanted him to stop. Pattie felt the tears in her eyes. She had never loved him so much as she did that night.

———

SUNDAY 26 MARCH

Pattie woke early the next morning to the grey light and the sound of rain. Mak was snoring gently next to her. The show the night before had been a success, and he was still sleeping peacefully. She brushed his hair from his eyes. She had watched his hair changed over that last ten years from a rich dark brown to a patchwork of grey and white. She would joke that he was turning into a hamster. It was getting long too, but it always suited him like that, curling around his ears. She wrapped a woollen shawl over her shoulders and sat quietly, watching him.

Last night, he had played so well. She had not heard him play or sing like that for years. He had new energy and enthusiasm, and the audience quickly caught on. Each song ended with real applause, not the half-hearted patting that sometimes happened as people raced to the bar for more drinks. She thought that perhaps Mak's career was not over yet. A few new songs to balance out some old standards and it would make a new album. A bit of marketing and this could just be the start of a solo career. Gentle encouragement, she thought.

She had recorded last night on her mobile so that Mak could hear it later. A better recording of the next gig would give him some material to consider and some ideas to send to the record company. The landlord was pleased. Mak on his own would cost less than Mak with the rest of the band.

Mak was starting to stir. She could feel him stretching out. His leg brushed hers, and she could feel his muscles still firm and taut. His skin was paler that hers and sometimes it had a sheen that used to glow under the spotlights, making him look almost luminous. Then he opened one eye and looked at her.

'Hello, beautiful. Did I do good?'

'You certainly did.'

'So do I get a reward?'

'I'll go make some coffee. You want your breakfast in bed?'

Mak reached out his arms and pulled her back under the duvet.

'Yes, please, breakfast in bed.'

Pattie giggled as he wriggled down her body, kissing his way to her nipples. She was bed-warm and soft, and he wanted her. She stretched out her arms to the sides and arched her back, inviting him to go lower. Mak was in no hurry. He felt very good, and he thought that he might just relax and enjoy this. He wasn't sure, but he thought he might be getting hard. That would be amazing. At last. He had not managed this for a very long time.

Gently, he massaged Pattie's breast and then slid his hand down her thighs. Pattie moaned and ran her fingers through his hair, massaging his scalp as she pushed him gently down to between her legs. Mak's body responded, and he felt he was finally getting hard. He gently teased Pattie's cunt, feeling her get wetter and wetter between his fingers.

Then, suddenly and quite unexpectedly, he pulled himself up and placed his firm penis inside her. Pattie's eyes opened wide with surprise. They looked at each other with delight as Mak started to move slowly. Pattie's hips relaxed, and she slid her knees up higher. Neither spoke as they lost themselves in each other. It was gentle, and when the climax came, both were still looking at each other with eyes wide open. The moment they shared was theirs alone. The rest of the world had just disappeared. Mak finally collapsed onto Pattie's breasts, and they both lay very still, not wanting the moment to end. Pattie kissed the top of his head, and the tears of relief ran down her face.

After a long silence, Mak looked up.

'Crying is forbidden in my bed, Pattie Harding.'

His voice was playful and full of happiness.

'I shall think you don't love me if you do that.'

'Cos I don't love you, horrible man. I'm trading you in for a new model tomorrow.'

'Nooooo. Don't do that. I have all the working parts again, and that was just a demonstration of my new skills. Make me a coffee and maybe once my batteries are charged, I can show you some more of my superhuman powers.'

He squeezed her to him and pulled her on top of him, where they lay just smiling at each other.

'Got my mojo working, baby.'

'You certainly have.'

Pattie smiled and kissed the end of his nose, while her tears dripped on his cheeks.

———

SATURDAY 1 APRIL

The sun was warming up at last. Spring flowers were everywhere, and the foolhardy had already got their shorts out ready for the anticipated hot summer. KC kept his long winter coat on for now. His days could often drag on into the evenings and even all night if something were happening. He filed his final notes on the Delia Mason death and told himself that he was wrong to suspect Mak Mason of murder. It was an accident, quite simply. Whatever doubts he had could well be based on his feelings towards Pattie.

For the first time, his desire for a woman had interfered with his judgement. He decided on a new regime of exercise and good food. Life as a police inspector was not a healthy one. There were too many takeaways and quick snacks on the run. He planned to go swimming when he got an evening off and had even tried running a few times. The image of Pattie Harding catching her halo of hair as it blew in the wind still appeared in those moments between sleep and awaking. He did not go to the Leopard, even though he sorely wanted a night out and some live music. He knew at some point he would have to apologise to her, but she would see this as a renewed attempt to shake her confidence in Mak. So he left well alone.

April Fool's Day started badly. All over the country had been another spate of clown sightings; the most dramatic was a masked man holding a knife who jumped out in front of a group of children and then followed them to school. KC had cautioned his team to treat any threats towards the vulnerable very seriously and a couple of badly made-up drunken clowns had already spent a night in the cells. On April 1st by nine in the morning, they already had ten clown sightings to deal with. Finally, he and his team got out on the streets, and by lunchtime, they had four pathetic teenagers and one very strange elderly woman under arrest for threatening behaviour.

By the end of the day, the teenagers were collected by their parents after KC had sent the biggest uniformed sergeant to read the riot act to them. Three of the four left in tears and the fourth was yelling loudly about police brutality. The weird woman was collected by her daughter and taken home, smiling happily. She had enjoyed her day in the cells and had demanded tea and cake from the custody officer, who kindly sent out for some. Why she had decided to wear a wig with a Donald Trump mask and an orange track suit that day was as much a mystery to her as it was to everyone else.

KC finished his paperwork and then sat and watched the sunset over the town from the grimy window in his office. It was a lurid, toxic looking sunset; the red was like dried blood and the yellow the colour of rotting leaves. Everything here was polluted. He had a sense of things coming to an end. A world in which people dressed up as clowns to frighten or intimidate others was not a world he liked. It felt like everyone had lost any sense of community and togetherness. It was 'look at me' on social media, on the streets, every-where. No one just faded into the background anymore.

Everyone wanted to be a celebrity. No one talked, they just texted.

He had received a text as a few days earlier from his girl-friend. She was still in the Algarve and was not coming back. She said they were not right for each other and she didn't see any point in seeing each other again. She wished him well. He felt very little. He had hardly thought about her since he first met Pattie.

KC searched the online database and then downloaded a copy of the official police resignation forms. It was time to go.

———

THURSDAY 18 APRIL

The days passed quietly. Mak rehearsed some new songs, and Pattie did the final accounts for Dearests Dos. Then she considered what to do next. She wondered if she should take on a new client or find herself a part-time job in a local accountancy firm. Much would depend on Mak. Aunt Maud's house had lots of viewings so it should sell soon. Janis had taken on the task of clearing her Mum's house and disposing of Delia's things. In Pattie's opinion, Mak's daughter was showing herself to be surprisingly tough and assertive. Despite her new self-confidence, nothing would make Janis go into the kitchen where her mother had died, and she paid for a clearance firm to come in to do it after the police had left.

Once everything was sold, Janis and Joe would have some funds to work with, and Mak was considering splitting the proceeds from Delia's house three-ways, so the kids got a bit extra. The salon equipment was sold to the new tenant, and all over town, Amelia's Salon de Beauté announced 'Grand Opening', complete with apostrophes, on the bright pink posters. Delia Mason was spoken of with fondness and regret, even if her old clients were looking forward to a new hairdresser.

Right now, Pattie wanted to be with Mak all the time. They made love frequently, and she almost believed the clock could be turned back. They could start again and get it right this time. His solo sets were popular, and the rest of the band seemed relieved. Will, the bass guitarist, was doing one night a week with a country and western band, and Marilyn had reclaimed Peter for Saturday nights with the family. He was taking on more emergency plumbing work to get himself out of the house.

Pattie had seen nothing of KC and was grateful that he did not drop into the Leopard to hear Mak play. Many people were taking tough decisions about their future, thinking it was no time to stay in a country sliding into financial ruin and social division. As the weather got warmer and with summer approaching, people had more energy and no desire to face another Brexit winter.

It was a sunny day, so that afternoon, Pattie decided to walk into the town centre to get some shopping. A walk would do her good. Make her feel fresh. Mak was settling down in his music room to practice. The three layers of insulating carpet kept the sound from travelling too much, and Mak would sit on his stool next to the desk and play for hours.

Pattie stood in the doorway and listened to Mak, in his faded jeans or old t-shirt, with one foot up on his amp, rocking while he played. It was a good feeling listening to him now. The stress had gone from his throat, and his voice had a lovely honey-mellow tone. She listened until he stopped for a moment and then went over and wound her arms around the back of his neck and nibbled his ear.

'Get off, women. This is no way to treat a rock star.'

He smiled and looked up at her fondly. The slight orange flecks in his pupils were soft in the afternoon light from the window.

'Off to get your dinner. Anything you fancy, apart from me?'

'Just you and a bacon sandwich will do.'

They were quiet for a moment, enjoying each other's warmth and smell.

'Okay, Mak. I will be a couple of hours. Should be time for you to pen a couple of million-dollar hit songs.'

Mak smiled.

'Love ya, Pattie. Don't be long.'

They smiled at each other, both knowing a whole world of possibilities was opening up at last.

Pattie started for the town, walking quickly and enjoying the sunshine. She bought some meat and some fresh pasta and then wandered around the shops for a while. About 3pm, she reached the café a few streets from home, and as it was quiet, she went in and treated herself to a coffee and a pastry. All this love was making her content. She would have to be careful not to put on weight. She settled down with one of the glossy magazines.

Back at home, Mak took a break and stood looking out the window, savouring his glass of whisky. The writing was going well. He stretched his fingers and placing his whisky glass on top of the amp, picked up the guitar and continued playing. Occasionally, he leant across to the desk and made some notes. His mind was on his music, but the faint smell of Pattie's perfume lingered on his t-shirt. He must be a very lucky man to have a woman like her, and this time he would show her that he was not a hopeless failure.

The café door opened, and Pattie looked up at the jingle of the bell. KC went straight to the counter and ordered a coffee. He was obviously off duty, wearing a track-suit and trainers. He looked very fit. Pattie saw no way of avoiding him other than to leave, and she didn't see why she should go. He looked around for a table and, seeing Pattie, raised his eyebrows questioningly. Pattie nodded, so he sat down opposite her. Pattie waited for him to speak.

'How are you? Well, I hope.'

'Sure, we are both well.'

'And Janis and Joe?'

'Janis is taking charge now; she is very capable. Joe is quiet, but he looks better. Not so withdrawn as he was. He comes to dinner once a week; spends time with his father.'

'And you, Pattie? How are you?'

KC was fishing, and she was determined to keep the conversation neutral. She no longer felt anything towards him. Those old feelings were pure fantasy.

'I am fine. Mak's solo sets are going very well. We will be doing some live recordings next month during the show. Landlord's son fancies himself as a producer. It will give Mak something to take to the record company.'

'Good.'

Then they were silent. Pattie was sure he was just looking for an opportunity to turn the conversation back to recent events and she did not want that.

'Look, Pattie, I just want to apologise for the last time we met. There is no hard evidence that those deaths were anything other than accidents. I am sorry I suggested otherwise. My job makes me suspicious sometimes.'

She nodded.

'I would like to come and hear Mak one night if you didn't mind me being there? I won't intrude, just be in the audience.'

'Fine. I can't stop you, but people might comment if they see me sitting with a copper too often.'

'Sure. I don't want to annoy Mak, and I think that maybe I do that. I will stay at the bar.'

He wanted to say 'and watch your beautiful face from a distance', but such things could not be said now.

• • •

Mak poured another large whisky. The new song was coming along well. He would leave it for now and try a couple of instrumentals now that his fingers were nice and flexible. His old amp had still not been serviced, and he had an idea there was a bad connection somewhere inside. He pushed the patch cord firmly into his steel guitar and bent down and cranked the volume up loud on the amp. Most people were out shopping, so no one would mind a couple of loud numbers.

He started to play and was rapidly oblivious to everything around him. As he rocked back on the stool, his amp rocked forward and at the same time, the glass of whisky spilt over, pouring a stream of dark liquid onto the amp and the carpet. He swore and pulled the patch cord from the guitar quickly. He reached over to find a cleaning cloth on the desk. When he turned back, there was a sharp crack, and the amp was smoldering.

His first reaction was to grab his treasured guitar and race out of the room and place it in the hall. By the time he returned, the amp was in flames, and the whisky on the carpet was also alight. Mak needed something to smoother the flames, so he ran back into the hall to get a coat from the hall stand. He grabbed an old padded winter jacket and ran back into the room to try to stop the flames. He beat the jacket over the amp and the carpet. Suddenly the jacket was on fire too, and a spurt of flame shot up to the ceiling. Within seconds, the old polystyrene ceiling tiles were a sheet of flames and smoke and toxic fumes filled the room.

Pattie and KC sat quietly and drank their coffee without much conversation. Then, in the distance, the sound of a siren could be heard getting closer. Neither commented, expecting the sound to pass them by. But it didn't. The sound grew closer and then came to rest very close by. Pattie looked anxious. She stood up and walked to the window. Behind the row of houses, black smoke was rising from the block of flats.

157

When Pattie grabbed her bag. KC could not avoid seeing the terror on her face.

All she said was 'Mak!' and ran for the door. KC followed her and soon caught up and ran past her into the next street.

By the time they reach the flats, the sky was a sheet of orange flame, and the fire-crew were tackling the blaze with high-pressure hoses. A police car had arrived, and the officers in uniform and high-visibility jackets were moving people back. Acrid black smoke was pouring from the top floor of the flats, and people were running from the entrance holding children and pets; anything they could grab on their way out. Pattie froze with her eyes on the door, looking for him.

'Oh no, Mak, please, please.'

KC pushed forward to the cordon and watched the smoky haze increase as the fire came under control. Then he went back to Pattie. She was standing still with her eyes fixed on the scene in front of her. Neither of them spoke. Helpless, they just watched the smoke blow away towards the fading sun. Pattie did not move. She wrapped her arms around herself and her eyes looked blank and empty.

Finally, when things seemed calmer, and the smoke died down, KC went back to the cordon and showing his badge to the officer, ducked under the tape and approached the fire crew and spoke briefly with the fire officer. Then, with a fixed expression, he ducked back under the blue and white tape and walked slowly back towards Pattie. She would hate him forever now. He paused for a moment and watched her.

Pattie's eyes were fixed on the flats, her arms wrapped protectively around herself, holding herself to keep out the pain. He was searching to find the words to tell her, but he didn't need to. Pattie knew. She was frozen, unable to move or cry out as her whole world crashed around her. The man she had built her hopes and dreams on was gone. She would never hear his voice again. In her mind, Pattie was already packing her life into one suitcase and walking away. She watched him come towards her and saw him shaking his head. Then she dropped to her knees on the pavement, unable to stand and gave a heart-breaking cry of pain.

Across the town, the small grey birds flew up and headed towards the warm wind rising with the smoke. The sleek cat on the wall twitched his paws as he heard a key in the door. Silently, he disappeared into the next garden.

'Come in, please. This family home has not been on the market long, and it is very attractively priced for a quick sale.'

———

DISCOGRAPHY

Music has been my inspiration while writing this book. As you read the story, I hope the songs will bring back memories of sad or happy days of your life.

♦ *Set Fire to the Rain*
   Adele
   ♦ *Summer of Sixty-Nine*
   Bryan Adams
   ♦ *Stuck in the Middle*
   Steelers Wheel
   ♦ *Sharp Dressed Man*
   ZZ Top
   ♦ *Merry Xmas Everybody*
   Slade
   ♦ *Fairytale of New York*
   The Pogues
   ♦ *The Wind Cries the Blues*
   Teresa James
   ♦ *All Right Now*

Free
- *Hotel California*

The Eagles
- *Run Rudolph Run*

Chuck Berry
- *Rock Me Baby*

Various Artists
- *Blues in the Night*

Rosemary Clooney
- *Make It Rain*

Ed Sheeran
- *Blues on Holiday*

Susan Tedeschi
- *Nutbush City Limits*

Tina Turner
- *American Pie*

Don Maclean
- *That'll Be the Day*

Buddy Holly and the Crickets
- *La Bamba*

Ritchie Valens
- *Donna*

Ritchie Valens
- *Chantilly Lace*

The Big Bopper (JP. Richardson)
- *Walkin' After Midnight*

Patsy Cline
- *Hello Mary Lou*

Ricky Nelson
- *Pride and Joy*

Stevie Ray Vaughan and Double Trouble
- *The Dock of the Bay*

Otis Redding
- *I Love You Because*

Jim Reeves

♦ *Sound of Silence*
Disturbed
♦ *Road to Hell*
Chris Rea

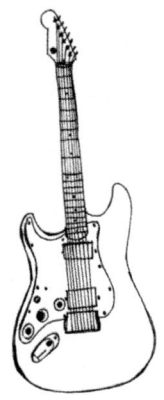

DEAR READER

Thank you for reading my book. You had so many choices and you chose me. I appreciate it.

Writing can be a lonely career, so I would be grateful if you could leave a review on Amazon – just some stars will do nicely. You might want to mention my book to your friends and family. Word of mouth recommendations help new readers find my books and help me to write more of them.

Please click the link to sign up for my Newsletter. I won't spam you or send so many emails that you hate me. That way, you will be the first to know when there is a new book for you to enjoy.

https://jansayer.com/

ALSO BY JAN SAYER

David Kettle finds a woman unconscious in the snow in his garden. Who is she and does he know her?

Time is running out and evidence is mounting up against him. Is David innocent or is he hiding something?

———

https://jansayer.com

Printed in Great Britain
by Amazon

11421845R00098

Socialism's Ignored Success: Iranian Islamic Socialism

Ramin Mazaheri

Badak Merah Semesta
2020

Socialism's Ignored Success: Iranian Islamic Socialism

Cover photos:
Diego Delso / CC BY-SA 4.0
Moeinashoori / CC BY-SA 4.0
Maryam Kamyab/Mehr News Agency / CC BY 4.0
Cover design:
Rossie Indira
Layout:
Rossie Indira

1st edition, 2020

Published by PT. Badak Merah Semesta
http://badak-merah.weebly.com
email: badak.merah.press@gmail.com

ISBN: 978-623-93644-6-5